DEAD MAN'S JOURNEY

Center Point
Large Print

Also by Les Savage, Jr. and available from
Center Point Large Print:

Long Gun
Shadow Riders
Lawless Land
The Teton Bunch
Outlaws of the Brasada
Satan's Keyhole
Buckskin Border

**This Large Print Book carries the
Seal of Approval of N.A.V.H.**

DEAD MAN'S JOURNEY

A WESTERN SEXTET

LES SAVAGE, JR.

CENTER POINT LARGE PRINT
THORNDIKE, MAINE

This Circle Ⓥ Western is published by
Center Point Large Print in the year 2019 in
co-operation with Golden West Literary Agency.

First Edition
August 2019

Printed in the United States of America
on permanent paper.
Set in 16-point Times New Roman type.

ISBN: 978-1-64358-303-7

Library of Congress Cataloging-in-Publication Data

Names: Savage, Les, author.
Title: Dead man's journey : a westen sextet / Les Savage, Jr.
Description: First edition. | Thorndike, Maine : Center Point Large Print,
    2019. | Series: A Circle V western
Identifiers: LCCN 2019019505 | ISBN 9781643583037 (large print :
    hardcover : alk. paper)
Subjects: LCSH: Large type books. | GSAFD: Western stories.
Classification: LCC PS3569.A826 A6 2019 | DDC 813/.54—dc23
LC record available at https://lccn.loc.gov/2019019505

Table of Contents

The Wagon Warrior   7

The Man Who Tamed Tombstone   63

Bullets and Bullwhips   145

Owlhoot Maverick   187

Bullets Bar This Trail   223

Dead Man's Journey   249

THE WAGON WARRIOR

I

David Brooke made a bizarre figure, sitting his split-ear pony there on the fringe of Council Grove where the wagons were gathering for the Santa Fe Trail. He looked more Indian than white, a short bow across his mount's withers, a quiver of arrows on his bare back. He wore his black hair braided over one shoulder like a Cheyenne buck's, and there was something hawk-like in his dark, aquiline face with its high cheek bones.

Most of Brooke's youth had been spent in the teepees of the Cheyennes. He was a brave, the deep scars on his chest marked him as having endured the Sun Dance. And he was blood brother to Chief Little Elk. Yet, when Becknell opened the Santa Fe Trail in 1821, Brooke had drifted back to his own people, the Yankees, acting as buffalo hunter for their caravans every spring, keeping them supplied with hump-rib and back fat all the way from Council Grove to Santa Fe.

This was a bad year for the Trail. Trains had been systematically raided through the preceding springs of 1837 and 1838, and there were Yankees who said the raider chief was Little Elk, violating the treaty he and the Osages made with the Americans at this very grove in 1825. Brooke had just come from his Indian brother's camp on the Neosho, and he knew how false this rumor was. But what weight would his word bear, who had smoked so many long pipes with the Cheyennes?

There was the other story, of course, to account for the raids. It was almost a legend by now, and only the old-timers and the Indians listened to it. It was a tale passed across the campfires. It was of *Los Diablos*—The Devils—a band of mysterious renegades who rode from the jagged Sangre de Cristo Mountains north of Santa Fe, raiding as far south as Mexico, as far east as the Missouri.

Even though the old-timers listened to the legend, they laughed after it was told, for it was only one of many, and they said it came from the influence of the awesome prairie nights or the eerie howl of a lonely loafer wolf when the coals were burning low. . . .

So it was a bad year for the Trail, and for the young hunter who was both white and red, sitting his buffalo pony there under the straight ash trees and thinking that he had never seen so many greenhorns gathered in one place.

A big solid-trunked man was picking his way through the Conestogas toward Brooke. He wore a gaudy, fringed buckskin jacket and a black soft-brimmed hat. He was Harvey Mohan. Behind him were the inseparable Georges Tremaine and Pinkie Haller.

Brooke felt his face grow carefully impassive as Mohan stepped across the last wagon tongue and put a thick-fingered hand on the pony's neck.

"Hello, Injun boy," he grated. "What you doin' at the Grove?"

There was a nasty inflection to Mohan's voice that made Brooke sit his mount for a long moment, not answering. He had never liked Mohan. The evident bull-strength in the man's body was turned brutal by the ugly twist to his sensuous-lipped mouth. The intelligence flickering behind his heavy-lidded eyes held a tight leash on that brute in him, and it made him doubly dangerous.

Finally Brooke answered, flatly. "You know what I'm doing here, Mohan. I run meat for the trains every year."

Georges Tremaine moved in from the other side, thin face leering. He was a Creole, and somewhere he had learned to use a gun too well, and he had excellent reasons for being so far from his native city of New Orleans.

Mohan curled his fingers into the horse's mane. "I'd advise you not to run any meat this year, Brooke. There's hardly an old-timer in this caravan. All tenderfeet from the East and hicks just off the farm. Would you want the responsibility of all them greenhorns on your back when the Injuns start raidin'?"

Pinkie Haller was by Brooke's knee, now. The

11

hunter felt his palm grow moist against his short hickory bow. Haller was a degenerate trapper whose only claim to fame was that he'd been scalped by some Kaws and had lived to tell the tale. He wore a greasy kerchief over his skull, but those who had seen him without it said they understood why he was called Pinkie.

A thin anger cut through Brooke, and his voice was very soft, almost inaudible. "I'd like to find the wagon master, if you'll step aside."

They didn't step aside. Haller's dirty hand slid toward the big Green River knife he had slung between his shoulder blades by a rawhide thong around his scrawny neck. Brooke knew his skill with that blade.

"Injun boy," said Mohan, "I been out here on the frontier a long time. Most folks know me well enough to listen to my advice. Those that don't listen usually find they should have. And I'm advisin' you not to go with this train."

Tremaine's hand looked very small and pale, hanging so close to the dragoon revolver holstered about his slim hips. Haller's hand was now splayed out on his shoulder.

Deliberately, Brooke slipped his knee from the hair rope about his horse's barrel. He placed his moccasin carefully against Mohan's solid chest and pushed hard. The big man sat down, wheezing.

Tremaine's hand was a white, dipping blur.

12

Haller snaked his blade from its thong with practiced ease. Then they stopped like that—the Creole with his dragoon not quite free of leather, the trapper with his wicked skinning knife still behind his neck.

For they were staring down the slender shaft of a long-headed arrow, nocked into the bowstring that was pulled back to Brooke's ear. And in the hunter's hand were six more arrows.

"Now," said Brooke with that deadly softness, "if you will step aside, I'd like to find the wagon master."

None of them had actually seen him draw those arrows. Yet there he sat, ready to let fly. And it was an axiom on the frontier that a skillful bowman could have his sixth shaft in the air before his first one struck its mark. A man was more likely to fall with half a dozen arrows in him than with one.

That was why Haller and Tremaine moved so carefully away, eyes fascinated by that nocked willow shaft. The Creole's gun made a small sound, rasping back into its holster.

But before Brooke could guide his quivering split-ear through them with a pressure from his knees, a young voice snapped out behind him.

"Drop your bow, Mister Brooke. You're under arrest!"

For a suspended instant the hunter sat with his bowstring still drawn, feathered arrow against his brown cheek. Then he lowered it, turning to face the man behind. Kansas sun slanted down through the ash trees, glinting on the blond head of a cavalry lieutenant who forked his big gray in the very middle of Council Grove Creek. His right hand rested on the service pommel, fisted around a big Walker model dragoon.

Brooke kept his voice even. "Under arrest, Hernic? Why?"

Hernic was a shavetail not long out of West Point, and his youthful arrogance sat heavily upon him. "I don't know that I'm obliged to explain anything, but Ballard's early train was wiped out. We found the remains only a few days ago on Turkey Creek. Only a few charred embers left of the wagons. I don't need to describe the bodies. We have orders for the arrest of Little Elk's band. I've been at Leavenworth long enough to know that includes you."

Mohan spoke then, and, turning, Brooke saw that he had been standing there quietly, taking it all in, eyes smoldering.

"Shippin' this Injun back to Leavenworth is the smartest thing you could do, Lieutenant," grated the thick-thewed man. "He spent the winter with Little Elk. I wouldn't be surprised if he took some of those Ballard party scalps hisself."

Brooke's hand twitched a little; that was the only sign of the impotent anger burning at him.

Lieutenant Hernic answered Mohan coolly.

14

"Unfortunately, Leavenworth is a hundred and thirty-eight miles behind us. I'm to provide escort for this train as far as Choteau's Island, and I can't spare any men to take Brooke back. He'll have to come with us."

Disappointment slid through the triumph in Mohan's ugly-mouthed grin. The lieutenant splashed out of the ford, holstering his dragoon and nodding indifferently for one of the troopers following him to pick up Brooke's bow. A pair of cavalrymen sidled their long-legged grays one to either side of the hunter, accouterments rattling.

Steadying himself with a slow breath, Brooke kneed his pony forward, Hernic's broad young back swaying before him, the rest of the troop cantering behind. And the last Brooke saw of Mohan, the man was staring after him with a black hate stamped into his heavy-boned face.

They picked their way through the motley collection of wagons, passing a gigantic Missouri teamster in red wool shirt and square-toed boots who was swearing at his stubborn mules with a profanity that approached a fine art. Farther on was a family making a poor job of loading their big Pittsburgh. It wouldn't be long before the trail jolted everything loose, and they would have to repack.

Finally Hernic halted them by a big red and blue Conestoga, red tassels hanging from the hames of each mule. Brooke saw the source of such pathetic display when the girl came around from behind the wagon box, smiling up at Hernic. She had thick hair like dull gold, and there was a depth to her blue eyes. Her crinoline was starched and gay. Brooke knew just how long that fresh dress and those tassels and all the gaudy red and blue paint would last.

Behind the girl swaggered a big, black-haired man. The strength of his big shoulders and the fine straightness to his long legs was spoiled by the dissipation in his florid face, the shiftiness of his bloodshot eyes.

"I'm Louis Walters," he said. "Wagon master. This is my fiancée, Julie Kerr. I was expecting you, Lieutenant."

Hernic swung down from his gray with too much flourish, bowing gallantly to Julie Kerr, then turning to the wagon master. "Sorry to trouble you, Mister Walters, but I'm afraid I'll have to put my prisoner in your wagon. It will be first in line, you see, and I want to keep a close eye on him."

The girl's glance toward Brooke was a mixture of disgust and scorn, and perhaps a little fear. "I won't have a red Indian in my wagon. Louis, tell them I won't have it!"

Hernic made his laugh soft for her: "He's a white man, despite his looks, ma'am."

Enough of Brooke's anger had disappeared so that he could turn to the girl and say, very gravely: "I can assure you I never scalp women with blue eyes."

She gave a startled gasp. Her widened eyes gazed for a long moment straight into his. Then she realized she was staring and lowered her face, flushing.

Hernic shot Brooke a frown, then turned to his sergeant. "Donahue, put this man in irons and keep a guard posted by the wagon at all times."

Donahue's face was a brick-red that came from a thousand long scouts, and as Brooke slid from his pony, holding out his hands for the manacles, he marked the non-com as being the first experienced man he had seen in this whole caravan.

Julie's father, Steven Kerr, had been a well-known trader on the frontier, having built up a large outfit through shrewd but honest dealing. When he contracted malaria in St. Louis, his daughter came from New York to nurse him. At St. Louis, Walters wooed and won her, but before they could marry, Steven Kerr died. It was typical of Julie that she should take the reins of her father's established trade, and insist on accompanying the wagons on their annual trip to Santa Fe.

Brooke couldn't help overhear the girl tell this to Lieutenant Hernic as the two sat outside the Conestoga after supper.

That afternoon the greenhorns had gathered beneath the stately Council Oak, choosing

17

for their leader the inexperienced, shifty-eyed Walters, because he owned the majority of the train. His wagons, and Julie's, combined, made up twenty of the thirty-four. He had to have lieutenants and a sergeant of the guard and a court, of course. And for some inexplicable reason, those greenhorns chose as first lieutenant, Harvey Mohan.

That troubled Brooke. Mohan was a wealthy man, supposedly owning controlling interest in the Rocky Mountain Fur Company. But in all his wanderings, Brooke had never met a trapper who knew of Mohan's connection with Rocky Mountain Fur. Again, if Mohan's source of wealth was trade with the Mexicans, Brooke had never seen any of the man's wagons in the Santa Fe trains, and he certainly owned no wagons in this caravan.

Brooke remembered, too, that look of naked hatred he had last seen on Mohan's face there by Council Grove Creek.

II

They rumbled out of the grove with dawn mist still swimming through the ashes and elms, and they stretched out with the inevitable cracking of whips and raucous cursing of Missouri mule-skinners.

Diamond Springs was some fifteen miles west of Council Grove. They made the green-grassed encampment by pushing on after dusk. Julie Kerr brought Brooke's supper with a hesitance in her step, making sure Hernic had posted his guard before she called the hunter out.

He slid from the tailgate, accepting the tin plate of hardtack and bacon silently, leaning against the rear wheel.

Finally the girl gathered her courage. "How . . . how did you come to live with the Indians?"

"My mother died when I was baby," he said. "My father was a trapper. We were in Green River country when the Sioux killed him. They traded me to the Cheyennes. I was about ten at the time."

Those scars on his chest drew her fascinated gaze, and he laughed wryly. "That's the Sun Dance . . . the way a Cheyenne becomes a warrior. The medicine man slits each pectoral with a bone knife. He puts hickory skewers through the slits and ties rawhide thongs to the skewers. Then they hang you off the ground and let you kick till the skewers tear from the flesh. Sometimes takes days. Then you can wear an eagle feather."

She fled with a horrified gasp, skirt swishing angrily toward the campfires. He put his head back and laughed softly.

When Sergeant Donahue came to check Brooke's manacles before retiring, his brick-colored face had lost its look of Irish humor.

"I can't understan' it," he growled. "This train had plenty of scouts and plainsmen to start with. They're just meltin' away beneath us. A party of trappers quit back at Council Grove when they'd promised to come as far as the mountains with us. An' tonight, Beavins and his Delaware hunters have disappeared."

"How many experienced hands does that leave?" asked Brooke.

"Billy Booshway and Tom Thorpe for scouts. An' mebbe a half-dozen teamsters in Miss Kerr's pay who've done the Trail."

Brooke knew Booshway and Thorpe, older men, faces seamed like worn rawhide, bodies fine and hard from years on the plains. He lay back on his buffalo robe beneath the wagon, wondering if Beavins and his Delawares had been taking Mohan's advice when they left so suddenly.

The prairie west of Diamond Springs was becoming criss-crossed with buffalo trails that marked the rank grass in a weird pattern. Here were the first antelope, and prairie hens began to flush from beside the Trail. Lost Springs passed behind. The timber changed, box elders and willows taking the place of ash and pignut hickory and maple. Crumbling bones of buffalo began to appear, hoary flaking horns marking where hunters or wolves had thrown their prey.

But it was all the same to Brooke, sitting there

in the swaying, creaking bed of the lead wagon, nostrils filled with the stench of the tar bucket.

It was customary to grease the wheels every morning with the dope from that tar bucket, a mixture of tallow, rosin, and tar. But these tenderfeet neglected it half the time, and were forever having hot boxes, their overheated wheels sticking and jamming and causing a delay almost every day.

Only Julie's teamsters seemed to know their business. Walters's men were as inexperienced as he with their outfits. They didn't watch their tires, and as the days grew hot, Brooke waited for the wheels to begin collapsing completely.

They were past the Devil's Hindquarters when the first one came apart. A lighter Murphy freighter suddenly dragged to a halt with a terrible squealing sound, its rear tire a dozen yards behind, its wheel crushed beneath the high-sided box.

A towering Missourian named Tahrr drove the wrecked Murphy, a giant of a man with tremendous shoulders beneath his red wool shirt. He and several others unloaded the wagon to lighten it. Someone rolled out a spare wheel. And Tahrr produced a solid piece of timber from beneath the running gear. He shoved a big packing box up to the wagon box, laying the hickory pole across it with one end under the Murphy. Then he and another muleskinner tried to lever the wagon up high enough to fit the wheel on, grunting and straining and cursing.

They had failed twice when Brooke slipped over the tailgate of his Conestoga prison and sauntered back, blue-coated guard following. Tahrr and the others were making a third try as Mohan stomped up, taking off his buckskin jacket. He shoved the gigantic Missourian aside indifferently.

"Hell! Let a man git at this," he growled.

The Murphy was not as large as a Conestoga, and it was empty. Still there was plenty of wagon there. None of them realized exactly what Mohan was going to do at first. He set his thick legs into the ground like oak trees, heavy-fingered hands gripping the axle. His face grew red. Cords snapped and popped in his big wrists, the muscles of his forearms writhed like fat hairy snakes. And that wagon rose.

"Git that wheel on, dammit!" he roared. "Git it on!"

The stunned teamsters scrambled for the wheel, mouths sagging. And when they'd fitted it over the axle, Mohan stepped back, breathing heavily. He caught Brooke watching him, and laughed thickly.

"Injuns ever teach you that 'un, Brooke?"

Brooke smiled thinly. "No, Mohan, not that one. But a lot of others, a lot of others."

Their gazes locked—two men who had different kinds of strength and who understood each other very well.

Turkey Creek was their camp on the seventh night, a place of fetid, steaming bottom lands where the mosquitoes swarmed into camp, turning it to a buzzing madness. Brooke sat close to a fire of buffalo chips, head in the stinking smoke, eyes closed. Around him he could hear the soldiers and teamsters slapping and cursing continually. Hernic passed, dignity imperiled by the red, swelling blotches on his handsome face.

"What the devil are you doing, Brooke?" he snapped.

The manacled hunter laughed. "The mosquitoes can't stand the smell, Lieutenant. You should try it."

Hernic snorted and stamped away. In a few minutes Donahue came over and sat cross-legged beside Brooke, holding his head in the smoke a long time before speaking. Finally he said harshly: "Billy Booshway and Tom Thorpe have disappeared!"

"Not exactly disappeared," said Mohan from directly behind. "They're bringin' in the bodies right now."

Brooke rose with no lost motion, not caring to remain seated with Mohan there. But the big man was already walking away, surprising grace to his movements. Brooke and Donahue followed to where a crowd had gathered. Georges Tremaine and Pinkie Haller sat their mounts in the middle of the noisy men. Two other horses were beside them.

Booshway and Thorpe lay across their saddles, heads hanging down one side and still dripping with blood from the scalping. The Creole was talking in his peculiar, French-flavored voice.

"We wair out 'unteeng on ze back trail, an' we fin' zees scouts zair."

"Yeah," said Haller. "Yeah."

Brooke looked closely at the slim Creole in his tight leather leggin's and fancy bolero jacket. The man forked a nervous horse, high-cantled California saddle double-cinched around its barrel.

"Do you hunt with your revolver?" asked Brooke suddenly.

The Creole's face tightened. "What?"

"I asked if you hunted with your revolver. You don't carry a rifle."

The crowd looked at that California saddle. There was no saddle gun booted beneath its broad hair cinches. And there wasn't much game to be had with a pistol in this country. The angry, frightened voices faded as Tremaine slid from his leather, black eyes narrowed and opaque. Brooke found himself in the center of strained silence. He had only to shake his manacles a little to know how helpless he was. But it wasn't in him to back down now.

Mohan stood alone in front of the crowd, an ugly leer on his face. He had only to wait and to watch, and when the time came, no blame would be on his head. Perhaps a lesser man would have pushed things. Not Mohan.

"I've never seen an Indian do such a sloppy job of lifting hair," said Brooke, wondering what he could do against that pale hand of Tremaine's. "Scalping does make a mess though, doesn't it, Haller? Did you wipe all the blood and hair from under your fingernails?"

Pinkie Haller responded automatically, bringing up his right hand to look at it stupidly. Perhaps Mohan hadn't figured that, perhaps he didn't want it to go any further. He waited no longer.

"He's sayin' you killed Booshway and scalped him!" shouted the big man, taking a prudent step backward. "He's callin' you murderers to yore faces!"

With a soft snarl, Tremaine uncoiled, right hand dipping and rising. Brooke had no time for reaction. He just saw that long barrel flashing upward and knew he was going to die.

The shot didn't come from Tremaine. It boomed out behind Brooke. The Creole jerked backward, twisting with the impact of a heavy ball in his shoulder, crying sharply and dropping his gun. Brooke turned to see Hernic standing there with his booted legs spread wide, a path in the crowd showing where he had elbowed through. His

25

big Walker still smoked in a steady hand, and his thumb was resting on the cocked hammer, waiting to see if Tremaine needed another slug.

Finally he spoke, lips against his teeth. "I think that would have been murder, Mohan. You take Tremaine to a wagon. I'll see you later."

He ordered Donahue to bury Booshway and Thorpe, then waved his gun at Brooke. The teamsters moved away from them as they walked toward Walters's Conestoga. Julie was on the outskirts of the crowd, her face white. She glanced at the two men, seeming to sense that this wasn't for her.

Hernic walked ahead silently, shoulders hunched strangely, jacking out the empty with a hollow clicking sound. At the wagon he leaned against the wheel, taking a deep shuddering breath. And for the first time, Brooke realized the boy was shaking.

At Brooke's glance, Hernic turned defiantly, spitting out his words. "Well, damn you, that's the first time I ever shot a man. The first time I ever stood there and squeezed out my lead and saw it knock him over backward with blood spurting."

Something tingled up Brooke's spine. Of course, of course. A kid, fresh from the Academy, where all they taught you was tactics and strategy and theory. Yet, there he'd stood, blond head thrown back and legs spread out wide, all cool and deadly, gun hand steady as a rock. The first time he'd ever shot a man. . . .

What a fire and a steel this boy had beneath his arrogance and his pride and his youth! Brooke put his manacled hands on Hernic's shoulder, saying quietly: "I was only fifteen when I shot my first man, Hernic, and after it was all over I went away by myself and cried."

The lieutenant looked at him, then straightened with an effort. "Well, it's done now, anyway. And there are other things. Booshway, for instance. How could you accuse a white man of scalping him?"

Brooke drew a heavy breath. "White men take scalps too, Hernic. It's just another thing you'll have to get used to."

Hernic was revolted. "But it's ghastly. And why should Haller kill Booshway?"

Brooke didn't answer directly. "You found Ballard's party on Turkey Creek, you said."

"Yes, about five miles north. Why?"

"If you'll ride out there with me, maybe we'll find out why Haller killed Booshway."

The moon cast a weird yellow-green glow over the rolling prairie. Hernic led the cavalcade on his big-barreled gray, Brooke following on his split-ear. Behind were four troopers, vainly trying to keep their sabers from rattling. It felt good to be mounted again after so long in that musty

27

Conestoga, and Brooke talked softly to his pony, smiling when one of the ears pricked up.

Ballard had evidently turned north, seeking an easier crossing than the usual one. The remains of his wagons formed dark splotches in the sandy bottoms beneath the fluttering talk of a willow copse. The bodies were gone, of course. Hernic had given them a Christian burial.

Brooke rode with no more saddle than a hair rope about his pony, through which he thrust his knees, the Indian way. He slid to the ground and kicked about through the charred ashes and pieces of burned wagon beds.

Finally he asked: "How many wagons was Ballard supposed to have?"

Hernic had come out here reluctantly and spoke with some impatience. "Twenty some odd, Brooke. I told you before."

"There aren't enough remains here," said the hunter evenly, "to account for more than three or four wagons."

Hernic's leather popped as he swung down, impatience wiped from his face. Brooke toed an iron tire with half-burnt orangewood spokes clinging to it.

"Not over a dozen tires. And look at those yoke irons, the bit-chains. Does this look like twenty wagons?"

"All right," said Hernic. "So the Indians took the other sixteen. Where does that leave us?"

"Indians don't take wagons," said Brooke. "You know that."

He began playing with his split-ear's mane, twining it in his fingers, and he looked out across the ghostly sweep of moonlit prairie with a strange set to his dark, aquiline face.

"Hernic, did you ever hear of *Los Diablos*?"

The boy's head jerked up sharply. "Now listen, Brooke . . ."

Brooke's quiet voice stopped him, going right on, as though the lieutenant hadn't spoken at all. "There was Weaver's train, for instance, in 'Thirty-Seven. He had a consignment of Hawkins muzzleloaders for Rocky Mountain Fur's agency in Santa Fe. Those rifles had carving on their stocks you couldn't miss. And he had a dozen pigs of Galena lead with his initials cut in 'em. His train didn't reach Santa Fe. A year later it was found by the Cimarron Crossing, the ashes, and what was left of the bodies. In that same year those Hawkins rifles turned up in Saint Louis. The pigs of lead appeared in Taos. It must be a marvelous organization, *Los Diablos*, to spread the loot that far."

Hernic swung an angry leg over his cantle, snorting. "I thought I was giving you a decent chance to help me, to prove you're more than the dirty red Indian you look. But I was mistaken. Now get on your horse. We're going, back!"

III

Beyond Turkey Creek the days were an endless monotony of broad spreading plains and squeaking wheels and stubborn mules. Once a herd of buffalo halted the train, migrating southward across the trail, a continuous stream of stupid beasts with small hocks and tremendous shaggy barrels.

Now and then the caravan passed a disused wallow, the stench of rotting frogs rising from its poisoned waters. The pale gold of diseased dodder mixed sickly with scarlet mallow about its rim. Even the shrill call of snipe held a hollow, mocking sound here.

Mohan rode the high box seat of a big, paint-peeled Pittsburgh most of the time. He never packed a short gun, but across his knees he held a heavy Sharps buffalo gun. Tremaine and Haller preferred their horses, though they kept close enough to Mohan. The Creole's shoulder was healing, but whenever he looked at Brooke or Hernic, a snake-like glitter entered his opaque black eyes.

And Brooke couldn't forget that he was the only plainsman left with the wagons now. All the others had disappeared, in one way or another. Tremaine had tried eliminating him once. Perhaps

Mohan wouldn't want the next attempt so noisy. That thought made Brooke watch Pinkie Haller closer—a Green River skinning blade carried no sound in its death.

Scudding gray clouds hid the sun on the day they reached the Big Bend of the Arkansas. Walters corralled the train in a swale between two humps of sandy ground, grown over thick with stunted cottonwoods.

Brooke climbed stiffly from the Conestoga and was leaning against a wheel when Julie brought supper. She kept glancing nervously toward Mohan's campfire. Walters was there, talking loudly, thickly.

The girl had lost some of her contempt for Brooke, some of her fear, and now she gave him the plate with a forced smile, saying: "Louis was all right for a while, when he'd drunk up all the Monongahela rye he brought from Westport. But now Mohan's started feeding him trade whiskey, every night."

"Oh," said Brooke. "Mohan."

She frowned, puzzled at the tone of his voice. Before either could speak again, Hernic walked past. He stepped over, bowing low to the girl. Brooke stopped eating.

"Lieutenant, I'm surprised you let Walters camp here. Hills on both flanks, thick timber coming right down to our wagons. Anybody could get right on top of your sentries before being seen."

31

Hernic faced him stiffly. "In the first place, it wasn't Walters's idea. It was Mohan's. He said it was close to water and the humps would hide our fires. And in the second place, I don't think you're in any position to be giving advice. Good night." He turned on his heel.

The girl watched him walk away; a small, amused smile curving her rich mouth. Then she murmured: "He's so terribly young, so terribly proud."

Brooke hardly seemed to hear her, and he might have almost been talking to himself. "Mohan has his hand in a lot of pots lately. . . ."

She looked at him sharply, but Brooke had his face turned toward those hummocks of sand, rising somberly on either side. A wind soughed through the cottonwoods. Their ghostly rattle held a foreboding.

Brooke was wakened that night by Sergeant Donahue. The Irisher came from outside the wagons, and his hoarse voice was a tocsin ringing through the fog of Brooke's slumber.

"Turn out. Indians. Turn out. Indians. . . ."

Over and over, not excited or afraid, just flat and continuous like the beat of a drum. Brooke rolled from beneath the Conestoga. Already his ears were filled with the sullen thunder of the cavayard being stampeded out beyond the corral. Troopers and teamsters were jumping

32

from their blankets, still groggy and confused.

Before Brooke could move in any direction, a dark blurred stream of riders burst through the wagons, leaping tongues and smashing up under high box seats, one after another until they swam before his eyes. Their gunfire opened up like flame that burned half a dozen stunned teamsters into the ground.

Brooke lurched around the Conestoga, almost knocking over Walters. The big man grabbed at him, panting: "Get me out of this, Brooke. Get me out."

The lean hunter shouldered him aside, catching Julie as she jumped from the wagon. Perhaps if she had thought, she would have clung to Walters in her sudden stunned fear. But she didn't think. She followed Brooke automatically when he took her by the hand.

The raiders were sweeping back and forth through the corral, the pound of their hoofs deafening, the blue-red flame of their gunfire blinding.

Brooke chose a gap in that swirling madness of flying manes and tossing heads, stumbling over the bodies of four soldiers where they had tried to form under a corporal. A Yankee trader was on his hands and knees, cursing bitterly, sinking a little lower with each oath.

A line of horses clattered by. Brooke threw Julie to the ground, falling deliberately on top of her, his body a shield. Slugs thudded into the ground about them.

Then he was up again, hunting in that smoky hell for Hernic, because the boy had the key to his manacles.

Hernic was backed against a wagon, blond head thrown up. There was awful deliberateness in the way he kept cocking and firing, cocking and firing, spilling saddle after saddle with deadly effect. All the arrogance and pride had left him. For that moment he was just a man who desired only to stand there and pump out his lead till he died.

As he stopped to reload, Brooke lurched up to him, bellying the smoking Walker down between them, shaking his manacles in Hernic's face.

"I've had these on long enough, Hernic, long enough."

Blinded by his battle lust, the lieutenant tried to shove Brooke aside. But the hunter twisted his arm, forcing him to where his saddlebags lay. Still struggling, the boy fumbled for the keys.

As he unlocked the manacles, Donahue and three troopers backed into the little open space of death Hernic had cleared with his dragoon. Walters staggered in, too, face twisted with fear. Behind him roared a pair of iron Missourians, brass-mounted Hawkins rifles bellowing. The rest of the corral was a carnage of dead and dying. Brooke and the others stood alone, the only ones left. And the raiders were reforming, wheeling, gathering for that last charge.

Hernic elbowed his way to the fore and would have stood there, jacking out empties and reloading and cocking and firing to the end. But Brooke had been taught in a different school.

He who fights and runs away . . .

The hunter grabbed Hernic, one arm crooked around his neck, the other twisting his gun arm. He yanked him off balance and pulled him back through the teamsters and troopers, back through the outspanned wagons. Donahue didn't have to be told when to retreat. He formed a masterly rearguard, waiting there in the breech with his three troopers until everyone was safe outside.

As that dark mass of riders broke into their sweeping charge, half hidden by a front of blazing gunfire, the sergeant pulled his men out. One of them dropped across a wagon tongue, coughing his life's blood into the shortgrass.

Brooke half-carried the lieutenant through the swamp grass of the river bottoms, talking to him in a low voice, almost as one would soothe a child.

"It's all over now, Hernic. You did what you could and they'd be proud of you back at the Academy, but it's all over now. There's no shame in running. Even Donahue understands that. . . ."

"The wagons!" choked Hernic, fighting. "Damn

you, I was sent to guard them. Let me go back, let me go back!"

Brooke pushed him into the mucky shallows. "I don't think we'll lose the wagons."

He ordered the others down, and they submerged themselves until only their heads remained above water, hidden by the willows. Walters was making a racket, shaking and sobbing and cursing. Brooke finally took Hernic's dragoon and crept over to the florid man, hitting him on the back of the head, neatly, coldly.

He collapsed into the water. Julie gasped at such brutality. Then she put her hand over her mouth, realizing why Brooke had done it. Riders had followed them into the bottoms.

For a long time those men cantered back and forth through the cottonwoods, calling softly to one another. Sometimes it was in Spanish, sometimes in English—never in Cheyenne.

But Brooke had hidden his party well, and finally the horsemen spurred back over the hump that separated the wagons from the river. Lying there in the cold water, Brooke heard muted sounds from over that hillock—the bawl of cattle, the faint calling of men. And finally the peculiar squeaking rumble of wagons beginning to roll.

Donahue took a heavy breath. "Lord, Lord, but that was a helluva business. I went out to change the guard on the cavvy, and find all the sentries lyin' in their own blood. When I come back soundin' the alarm, there was the guards on the corral in the same fix, knifed through the gullet."

"Someone stole our guns, too," offered a shivering trooper. "It wasn't nice, facin' them devils with our bare hands."

A steady drizzle had started when Brooke finally led Hernic out of the bottoms. He left the others behind, but he wanted the officer to see a few things.

The rain had put out the fire and there was enough of the smoldering wreckage to show that only three wagons had been left behind. Bodies were scattered in pitiful, grisly heaps. Hernic turned his head away from the sight—that singular, viscous look to the top of every head. It even made Brooke a little sick. But he forced the boy to help him, searching carefully through all the corpses. Mohan wasn't among them. Nor Georges Tremaine, nor Haller. And they couldn't find any bodies of the raiders.

"That proves they were Indians," said Hernic stubbornly. "They always carry away their dead."

Brooke kept his voice even with effort. "Indians don't attack at night, Hernic. They think a man who dies in darkness goes to hell. The only point in leaving burned wagons and scalped bodies is to throw the blame on the Indians. Do you think whoever did the raiding would leave their dead here to give the whole thing away?"

Hernic bit his lip, unable to meet Brooke's

37

gaze. That stubborn pride blinded him, made it impossible to admit he was wrong and the man he despised was right.

Ignoring him, Brooke hunted over the wreckage for any sort of weapon, but the camp had been stripped bare. Only a few buffalo guns lay amid the ashes, bent and broken and burned beyond use. He had to be satisfied with a hickory oxbow, only partly ruined. As he turned back toward the river a great gaunt figure in a red shirt stepped from the fringe of cottonwoods, covered head to foot by leaves and mud. Hernic had his gun out and cocked before he recognized the man.

"It was all over afore I was rightly awake," said Tahrr. "And I didn't hev no gun. So I buried muhse'f in the woods. Ain't no point in dyin', 'less you hev to."

"Tahrr," said Brooke grimly. "You are a man after my own heart."

IV

They marched all next day up the river, not very many of them in all that vast country, covered now by the dead gray blanket of rain that pelted down endlessly. Sometimes they sank to their knees in the sand and mud. A smoky mist swam through the mottes of soggy cottonwoods, lending an unreality to their pain and exhaustion.

The sergeant and two of the teamsters had guns, but they had used their last ball in the fight. The two cavalrymen who had escaped with Donahue were unarmed. That left Hernic's dragoon with three precious loads and Brooke's hunting knife as the only real weapons in the whole party

They made a forlorn camp under some elms. Brooke formed a bed of boughs for Julie, and set guards for the night. When he gave Donahue and Walters the two hours before dawn, the wagon master bridled.

"I'm still leader here, Brooke, and I'm not taking any orders from a half-naked savage."

Brooke's dark face became impassive—his voice took on that almost inaudible softness. "I'm going to try and keep you all alive out here, Walters. But if you get in the way, I won't have to be mad to kill you."

The infinite deadliness in those low tones made Walters take a fumbling step backward, surprise and fear blanching his face. And two hours before dawn he rose from his soggy bed of grass and mud to stand watch with Donahue.

The rain had stopped next morning. Brooke showed them where to find the tipsin root, and they chewed it during the weary march, gaining some nourishment. At noon they came across blackberries and a few plum thickets. And mile by mile they marched westward, barely warmed by a feeble sun, bitten by buffalo gnats that rose in swarms from the swampy bogs formed by the rain.

At the evening camp, Brooke began to carve on the hickory ox yoke, watching Hernic. The young lieutenant sat with his blond head in his hands, utterly defeated. He had failed in his command, had lost most of his men—and apparently didn't care whether he lived or died.

But Brooke remembered how Hernic had stood with his back against the wagon, facing that pounding, blazing death. Nothing could defeat a man like that, permanently. And when the Trail had polished off his arrogance and stiff-necked pride, the stuff beneath would be a thing to see.

So Brooke sat, patiently carving on the ox yoke that would eventually be a short bow as deadly as the one he had had before.

The next day he cut half a dozen willow withes from the riverbank and dried them in the sun. It was another day before they passed a rocky formation from which he could form arrowheads, and yet another before he flushed a wild turkey. He used one of Hernic's precious balls on the bird, and that evening while the others were still eating its meat, he set about to finish his arrows. He cut fringe from his buckskin leggin's and moistened it in his mouth, then slit the turkey feathers and bound them to the nocked end of the willow shoots with wet thongs.

Some of his arrows had broad short heads with

barbs to hold in the wound, and these were meant for hunting. Some had long slender heads without barbs, and these were meant for war.

Because he knew now that he wouldn't be satisfied with just leading these people to safety. A desire was growing within him to get those wagons back. It was almost something personal, between him and Mohan.

That was why he began teaching Hernic and Donahue and the soldiers and the teamsters how to live in this country and how to fight.

Donahue was short and stocky. He had a cat-like compactness that the towering Missourians and even the lieutenant lacked. So Brooke chose the brick-faced sergeant to teach the ways of the knife. At the end of each weary day, he showed Donahue how to block and how to stab, and how to kill. He taught the non-com all he had learned from Little Elk and the other Cheyennes, and he had learned a lot. Donahue was Irish, and pugnacious by nature, and he had a talent for any fighting. He learned fast.

The hunter taught the others, too. He showed them how to crawl through willows without disturbing a single shoot. He made them lie in bogs and swamps for hours on end without moving a muscle. Julie learned with the men. She had become one of them.

This was Indian country, of course, and one of the hardest lessons was learning to cover their trail. Sometimes they used rocks, leaping from one to the next, or walked across fallen timber to leave no footprints. And for days at a time, they used one of the oldest methods, walking in the shallows of the great brown sluggish Arkansas. So Brooke taught them.

Often they would grow so weary that he had to beat and fight and abuse them forward. He grew leaner, and his body came to look like a blade of a fine Damascus. His tensile strength went deeper than his body, though, and it became more apparent every day.

Wind wrinkles were beginning to appear around Julie's blue eyes; her hands were no longer soft. She cried at night, sometimes, when the day had been hard. Yet, she never complained. It was Walters who showed most strain. He had lost weight, his hands twitched a lot. He had been almost two weeks without liquor.

Brooke shot a black-tail deer, and made the girl a short Crow skirt from its hide, split up the center. She exchanged it willingly for her crinoline, torn and dirty and not meant for rivers or briars.

On the fifteenth day they were slogging through hip-high blue root near the Cimarron Crossing of the Arkansas. Orioles were singing from a grove of aspens that covered rising ground to the north. Suddenly the birds ceased their talk. Their wings made a soft whirring against the muted roil of the river.

Brooke stopped, moving his hand slightly. Those behind sank into the grass without sound as he had taught them. Then he squatted down, nocking an arrow with a long slender head into his hickory bow's string. He had known that sooner or later he would use those arrows for war.

In a moment, the first Indian appeared, riding from the trees. He forked a stallion, gray with small black Arab spots, the gaudy paint horse so dear to a red man's heart. Following were others, single file, cantering out of the trees like a line of gaily-mounted ghosts, eagle feathers nodding from black hair, red, blue, and yellow blankets wrapped around lean torsos. Brooke let his bowstring slacken and stood up. These were Cheyennes.

The riders suddenly became a swirling pool of wheeling mixing color, blankets flapping as they reared their ponies back on one another. But the brave in the lead had marked those Sun Dance scars on Brooke's chest. He threw himself from his mount, dropping his yellow blanket to reveal similar scars on his own body.

"You are a brother," he cried joyfully. "You are a brother."

Brooke greeted him, then turned slightly. Donahue and the others rose from the grass. Surprise flickered across the Cheyenne's painted face, and Brooke smiled a little. That the Indians hadn't spotted those lying in the blue root was the greatest of compliments, the final test, really. The hunter had taught his people well.

They were great lean greyhounds of men, these braves, and they had been north on a war party against the Blackfeet of the Big Horns. They had captured many horses and were in good spirits. When, as a brother, Brooke asked them for enough ponies to mount his party, they gladly gave him a dozen skittish little mustangs. The Indians had just killed a buffalo, and they shared hump rib with the whites. Brooke sat cross-legged by the fire, talking to them in their own language, and he had never looked more like an Indian. Finally he asked one careful question of the brave leading the party.

"Yes," answered the painted warrior. "A big wagon train passed us going north toward the mountains, but we let it alone. That is our treaty, you know, with the white man."

Brooke watched the Cheyenne narrowly. "Why should a wagon train be going north so far from the Trail?"

The Indian avoided Brooke's eyes not speaking. But finally he spat it out, half in anger, half in fear.

"Los Diablos."

He rose stiffly, jerking his head at his warriors. They mounted without another word, rounding up all but the ponies they had promised Brooke, and galloped off in a rising cloud of dust toward the river. Brooke stood watching them go, a small triumph in his smile. Then he turned to the others.

"Now that we have horses, it wouldn't be hard to reach Santa Fe. You'd be safe there. Or we could ride after the wagons. And some of you would die."

Hernic rose, a strange set look to his face. Perhaps he still disbelieved the existence of *Los Diablos*, yet Brooke knew he would give his life cheerfully for even the smallest chance of vindicating himself.

Tahrr spoke for the muleskinners. "I got a mule in that train named Peaches. I'd like to git muh hands on the critter whut stole her."

"And you, Julie?" asked the hunter.

"They're my wagons," flamed the girl, almost defiantly.

There was a sudden scuffle. Hernic slapped at his holster in a startled way. But Walters had the gun in his hand, eyes glittering insanely. Brooke had seen the look before. The Trail did that to some men.

"You didn't ask me, Brooke," babbled Walters in a high-pitched voice. "They're my wagons too, you know. And I say they can go to hell. You're taking us to Santa Fe, or I'll kill you!"

He cocked the gun with its two precious loads. The hollow click was the only sound. The others stood like graven images, knowing it would mean Brooke's death to make so much as a move. There was nothing the hunter could do. And if Hernic had his spread-legged, god-like way of meeting the end, so did Brooke have his way. He drew himself up a little, face impassive, and there was something infinitely proud in the thrust of his chin.

Perhaps Walters had expected fear. There was a puzzled hesitance to the way he thrust the Walker out before him, steadying it.

Julie took that moment to step in front of Brooke. "You'll have to use that first ball on me, Louis."

Then Donahue stuck his foot out and shoved Walters over it, and Hernic leaped for the big man's gun arm, and all the others jumped him like a pack of wolves.

The gun exploded. Tahrr rolled from the mass of struggling bodies, cursing hoarsely and holding his side. The fight lasted only a moment, arms flailing, feet kicking. Then someone groaned sharply from the bottom. The men untangled themselves. Donahue got up, panting. Hernic rose, holding his gun by its barrel. There was a film over his eyes, and he stood looking from the bloody gun butt to Walters's crushed skull.

Suddenly he dropped the dragoon in the sand, and turned to walk away into the night.

Donahue started to follow, but Brooke caught

his arm, muttering: "Let him go, Sergeant. He's young. . . ."

"Yeah," said Donahue. "Yeah, I guess you're right."

They did what they could for Tahrr's wound, and buried Walters in a shallow grave, piling rocks over it. Brooke stayed beside Julie when the others had left. She was dry-eyed, looking at the cairn dully.

"I guess I couldn't really have loved him," she said. "Because I can't feel much sorrow. He was handsome and he had a swagger. Those things go to a woman's head. But he was weak, wasn't he? He could never belong to this wild, raw, new country as you do, David. I don't understand you very well, yet. I'm just beginning to realize how strong you are."

They traveled fast now, on their horses. And Julie understood why Brooke had made that split in her skirt. The ponies were small, mule-hocked, with rasping hides and cockleburs in their sparse manes. But they were horses. They had an incredible endurance—a rawhide toughness that never wore out. Brooke rode a deer-legged palomino with taffy mane and tail, and soon he was talking to it in soft tones as he had talked to his beloved split-ear.

They found the wagon trail rather easily, running through the prairie somewhere north of

Choteau's Island. And they followed it, through spreading plains studded with prickly pear, over the spring prairies of eastern Kansas Territory that rose seven and a half feet to the mile—and suddenly they were in the mountains. Great shaggy mountains, covered with timber, pine and cedar and birch. The wagon ruts led into a broad valley for a day's march. Then, as the valley narrowed and the sun dipped low over the red peaks, that trail ceased.

Brooke slid from his palomino, leaving it to stand hipshot there in the blue-green buffalo grass. He started circling, head bent low like a hound on the scent. And finally he discovered the new soil. A kick with his worn moccasins revealed the trail, carefully spread over with fresh dirt.

That they should suddenly take such pains to hide their tracks gave Brooke the hope that he was near the legendary kingdom of *Los Diablos*.

Farther on he found some cherries lying on the ground where wagons had knocked them loose. And later, it was a slim birch, bark eaten partly away at the height of a mule's head. The mountains closed in, the timber thickened. Finally they reached a creek. The timber about it was so dense that Brooke knew the wagons could have followed no other trail than the water itself. He turned boldly into its level, sandy bottom, leading his band through the veritable tunnel of cedar and pine, with plum thickets forming an almost impenetrable wall beneath the trees on either side. The sun shone through, dappling the water eerily. A jay called.

If this were the entrance to the camp of *Los Diablos*, there would be guards. So Brooke dismounted half a mile up the creek and left the ponies in charge of Tahrr, whose wound was still troublesome. Then he led the others through the timber, set so close and grown with underbrush so thick that no horse could have penetrated it. Julie insisted on coming with them, and she fought her way grimly and silently through the briars.

They ascended a slope, and the trees thinned until they were walking through towering pines that reached up to the blue sky and sighed in the afternoon breeze.

Suddenly, through those straight trunks, they saw the valley. It was set like a cupped hand amid awesome peaks of hazy purple and red that surrounded it completely. A river ran down its center; on either bank grew cottonwoods, their leaves almost hiding the water and forming a broad band of fluttering gold clear across the jade-green pampas grass of the valley.

"It's beautiful, David," said Julie.

"And deadly," said Brooke, pointing to where smoke rose above the cottonwoods. *"Los Diablos."*

He felt no triumph or justification in the discovery, and he looked no longer at Hernic than he looked at the others when he said the words. It was just the end of the trail, that was all.

V

Brooke led down a spur ridge toward that rising smoke, and finally they stopped at the edge of the timber. Before them was the camp—the place of legend that no man but those who rode with *Los Diablos* had ever seen. The cottonwoods had been cleared, and a double row of log cabins set near the river. Farther back was a solid, pack-pole corral, filled with horses, and beyond that grazed a giant herd of cattle, spreading out over the valley. Parked north of the cabins were the wagons—Pittsburghs, Conestogas, Pennsylvanias, even some Red Rivers. Walters's wagons, Julie's, Ballard's—more wagons than Brooke had ever seen collected in one place.

A bunch of Yaqui Indians lounged in front of one cabin, half a dozen 'breeds in leather leggins and cowhide vests talked before another. A group of lanky trappers in 'coon hats and greasy elk-hides fished from the cutbank. Renegades from all races, gathered here and welded into a veritable army that could strike as swiftly and devastatingly as it had that night so long ago on the Arkansas.

Looking to where the river entered the valley, Brooke saw what he would have met had he taken the water route in. A dark knot of men gathered on the fringe of dense timber, low sun glinting on their rifles.

Hernic and the others must have realized, then, why Brooke had taken such pains to teach them his way of fighting—the Indian way. There would be no sweeping charge down the valley, with accouterments rattling and guidons flapping. Perhaps Hernic would rather have done it that way. But he had no guidons, no accouterments. Only a handful of exhausted wanderers and a short bow and a gun with one bullet. Donahue could contain himself no longer.

"Lord, Lord, what an outfit. It musta taken a mastermind to figure this up."

"Harvey Mohan has an intelligence, of a sort," said Brooke dryly.

Night was a blanket that hid the grim little file struggling up through the shadows beneath thick cottonwoods. A Mexican squatted against the wall of the first cabin, his *cigarito* a small glow in the dark. Brooke moved his hand slightly, and those behind him sank into the willows. Then he nocked a long-headed arrow to his string.

Any compunction he felt about killing the man in cold blood was swept away by the picture

51

of those bodies back on the Trail, that singular viscous appearance to the tops of their heads. These men had done that.

The smoker made no sound. He just slumped forward, the shaft quivering a little in him. Brooke snaked over to pull his arrow free, and to unbuckle the Mexican's pair of guns. He returned to the river, giving each of Hernic's two troopers a holstered revolver. One of them slipped his from its cowhide holster—one of Samuel Colt's newest models. He hefted it almost lovingly in his calloused hand. He had waited a long time for this. But Brooke wasn't ready to use those guns yet. He gave Donahue his skinning blade and told the sergeant to follow him into the valley.

They squirmed through the willows toward the big park of wagons, pupil moving as silently as teacher. Brooke rose at the first wagon, peering into its bed. Freight still bulked there, and it was the same in other wagons.

That was the safest way—to hold the stolen wagons here for a season until the memory of the massacres had died somewhat, then to sell the goods anywhere from Santa Fe to St. Louis. A fortune was tied up in this collection alone. There would be many men on the frontier willing to ride with *Los Diablos* for that kind of money.

Brooke stalked through the freighters, and caught a lone guard with his silent arrow. Donahue stayed beneath the bed of a Pittsburgh

52

while Brooke crept out to remove his shaft. He was unstrapping the man's hip gun when an expelled breath whirled him round.

Pinky Haller was easily recognizable in the moonlight, his Green Rivet knife already a glinting arc sweeping down at Brooke.

The hunter let himself collapse suddenly beneath that charge. The knife slashed past his shoulder. Haller followed it, thrown off balance, his body a sudden crushing weight on Brooke. It was a silent, bitter fight there in the damp grass. Haller was astraddle Brooke, with all the advantage. He caught the hunter's neck and struck again, up, down.

Desperately Brooke rolled to one side, warding the blade off with one arm, feeling it slash him from wrist to elbow. He kept jerking from side to side like that, throwing up one arm, then the other. Haller's face was twisted into a snarl, he panted with each vicious thrust.

Brooke was glad he'd brought Donahue along, then.

The bony trapper was suddenly jerked off him by the brick-faced sergeant, and the two of them heaved away into the grass. Brooke got to his hands and knees, breathing hard. He saw Haller rise up and strike. Donahue blocked. Then Donahue struck. Haller didn't block.

The sergeant stood up, grinning. "B'gorra, that's one for Billy Booshway."

Somehow Haller's greasy kerchief had been torn off, and the two men didn't look at him long because his skull was all pink and scarified and strangely revolting.

They killed four more men, getting their weapons. Donahue was loaded down with holstered revolvers and Hawkins muzzleloaders when they came to that fifth man. He was standing in the shadow of a big Pittsburgh, and Brooke's shaft didn't strike quite as true as it might have, and he made a lot of noise before he died.

Brooke and the sergeant hurried back to those in the river bottom, the camp already in an uproar, men running back and forth among the cabins, calling and shouting. The hunter was about to lead his party back down the river when he saw a stocky man lighted for an instant in an open doorway. He was thick-bellied and broad-hipped and he wore a gaudy fringed hunting coat. Harvey Mohan.

Brooke had proved himself deadly enough with his short bow to have sent half a dozen shafts through Mohan in that short moment; the big man stood silhouetted by the yellow light, a perfect target. Yet the hunter made no move to nock his arrow. It would have been too much like shooting a deer or a buffalo. This thing between him and Mohan had resolved itself into something far more personal and intense than that.

The big man moved off into the milling crowd, but everyone had seen him, and it made everything quite clear, even to Hernic.

It had been Mohan from the first, of course—discouraging Beavis and his Delawares, having Booshway and Thorpe killed, trying to get rid of Brooke. Mohan hadn't wanted any experienced men to face his *Diablos*, only a bunch of tenderfeet and a drunken wagon master and a green lieutenant.

Well, that lieutenant wasn't as green as he had been, and some of those tenderfeet were still alive, and Pinkie Haller would knife no more guards.

Brooke led his party downriver from the roused camp. They were well armed, now. Even the hunter packed a revolver, silver-studded belt rasping strangely against his bare hide.

The next morning Brooke sent Donahue and a trooper down to get Tahrr where they had left him with the ponies. Down in the valley, men were riding from the camp, in ones and twos, sometimes larger groups. They disappeared into the timber at the valley mouth, taking the river route, and none of them returned. Brooke well knew what it meant to those superstitious Indians, finding their fellows dead in the night with only a bloody hole in the chest to mark their passing. Fear was sapping Mohan's strength!

The hunter was still watching, when Donahue and the trooper suddenly appeared down on the slope, supporting Tahrr between them. Brooke ran into the clearing to help them.

"Some damned Yaquis found me," groaned the Missourian. "They took me to Mohan. Wuz gonna hang me by muh thumbs till I tol' whar you was. But I got loose. I think they follered me."

Yes, they'd followed him. A lesser man would have opened fire without warning, but Harvey Mohan had a bigness to his villainy. He stepped from the trees a hundred yards below, that Sharps across his square belly, *Los Diablos* forming a long line behind him.

"I knew it was you last night, Injun boy!" he yelled. "Nobody else coulda killed seven men so dead they didn't make a sound dyin', nobody else coulda led a bunch of tenderfeet through two hunnert miles of hell. I guess you must hate me just about as much as I hate you."

Tahrr gave Brooke his chance. The teamster lurched erect, bellowing in pure rage, and whirled to charge down the slope. Mohan and his renegades had been ready to open up on Brooke and the others. But it was automatic for them to turn their fire on that onrushing juggernaut in the red shirt. Tahrr jerked to the hail of lead through him, but he had a terrific momentum, and he had his rage, and he wasn't going to die until he got hold of Mohan.

Mohan dropped his rifle calmly, setting his oak-tree legs, bending forward with his arms out to meet that charge. He was the type to do it that way.

Tahrr thundered into him with a terrific crunch of bone on bone. Mohan shivered from head to toe, and he seemed to sink a little into the ground. But he didn't go over. Using Tahrr's own momentum, he lifted the giant far upward, slinging him back and over to hit with a sickening thud and to lie still.

Brooke had taken that chance Tahrr gave him, though, retreating up the hill with Donahue and the trooper, picking up Hernic and the others, and moving on up toward the ridge. The battle became a deadly thing then—flitting shadows and sudden thundering guns, and men dying without rightly having seen who killed them.

Somehow Georges Tremaine worked around to their flank, appearing suddenly on Hernic's end of the line, a bunch of Yaquis behind him. The lieutenant whirled to meet his charge.

"Zat blue coat's mine," called the Creole thinly. "Mine!"

Hernic threw his blond head back that way, spreading booted legs. And perhaps Tremaine remembered the other time he had faced this boy, for at the last moment he hesitated.

Hernic began firing, then, that cool, deliberate fire. Cocking and firing, cocking and firing.

Tremaine went down with a high, womanish cry, thin body flopping over and over until it brought up against a tree. But Hernic didn't stop shooting. His .44 bucked and bucked and bucked, knocking down men with thundering precision.

The Yaquis wavered, just as Tremaine had wavered, and they broke and ran. Hernic stood there with his smoking Walker canted down a little, looking at the men he'd killed. There was no film over his eyes now and he wasn't shaking with reaction.

Then Mohan broke through the timber below, dropping one of the teamsters, and Brooke began his steady retreat again. Suddenly they were on the ridge. Brooke called Hernic to him.

"We've held the advantage by being above. I don't want to lose it by moving down the slope behind us. You take your troopers and the muleskinner and flank Mohan. Do a better job on him than Tremaine did on us."

Hernic moved off, gathering his men, disappearing into the timber. Brooke leaned against a tree, shoving new loads into his dragoon.

"Julie," he said. "Keep a bullet for yourself."

She nodded gravely, eyes glistening a little. "I'll be proud to die beside you, David."

Donahue was loading his pair of dragoons carefully. He would give an account of himself. *Los Diablos* were nearing, not so many as before, perhaps a score. Mohan led, walking with that strange grace of his. And the rush came suddenly, a hell of screaming men and blazing guns.

Brooke tried to nail Mohan, but gun smoke hung thickly through the trees hiding him. And there were others. A Yaqui erupted through the haze, dark face contorted. Brooke shot him in the belly. A Mexican lurched into the hunter's sights. Brooke shot him in the face. Another few seconds and Hernic's flanking charge wouldn't do any good.

A big trapper knelt to fire at Brooke, his slugs chipping bark into the hunter's face. Brooke's slug caught him square and he went over backward. Then that dragoon was empty.

Hernic struck suddenly, careful fire dropping half a dozen *Diablos*. He came on in, and they couldn't face that surprise from the side. They scattered back down the hill, the lieutenant hot after them with his flaming Walker.

But Mohan hadn't run. Brooke saw him suddenly, all alone now, still moving up the slope in a steady, solid-footed jog trot. Coming for Brooke, coming for the lean, brown sword blade of a man who'd defeated him so utterly. Not hurrying especially, just coming, grimly, inexorably. Donahue was on his hands and knees, blood forming a pool between his splayed fingers. And Julie hadn't saved that last ball for herself. She was vainly trying to reload.

Brooke dropped his empty revolver, a burning

59

exaltation sweeping through him. He knew now why he hadn't shot Mohan from ambush last night. Because this was the way it should be, the way it had to be—he and Mohan, face to face. The other man was nearer, big buffalo gun held at hip-level, swinging a little with each deliberate stride. Brooke raised his bow with an arrow nocked, and pulled his gut string back smoothly.

Mohan didn't even break his stride, just fired from the hip, still coming on. With the terrific jar of the .50-caliber slug driving him to his knees, Brooke loosed his arrow, straight, true. Waves of sick pain blinded him momentarily. Then he could see again.

Mohan was still coming and it was terrible to see. A big, square-bellied man, his awful bull-strength and his implacable hatred driving him on, even with an eighteen-inch willow shaft buried deeply into his thick chest.

"David," shuddered Julie. "He won't stop. He . . . won't . . . stop!"

The hunter fought a roaring pain that threatened to sweep him away, and he raised his short bow again. It was an axiom on the frontier that a skillful bowman could have his sixth shaft in the air before his first had struck its mark. . . .

Brooke's arrows thudded into Mohan like the swift beat of a tom-tom. The first one didn't even stagger him. The second made him grunt sickly, but he kept right on coming. The third, the fourth, the fifth. But as the last one drove home, he stumbled, took a final step, and fell on his face.

Even then he didn't stop. With an awful effort of will, he began to crawl forward, hands digging into the earth, spasmodically. Brooke was unable to move. He just crouched there on his knees, watching Mohan, fascinated.

Blood bubbled from the other's mouth. He rose, thick fingers clawing out for Brooke. Then he collapsed, dead. The heads of those six arrows protruded from the broad back of his gaudy, fringed hunting coat.

And a man was more likely to fall with half a dozen arrows in him, than with one.

They put Donahue and Brooke in one of Julie's Conestogas, setting out for Santa Fe that same day. The sergeant was a sieve, but hanging grimly to life with all the stocky strength of him. Brooke's wound was a clean one, though his hip felt numb, pain running through him whenever the wagon jolted over a rock in the river bottom. He lay there in the musty interior, able to see Hernic and a trooper where they sat, spelling each other on the reins. Julie sat beside Brooke, and she caught his eyes on Hernic's back.

"A few weeks ago"—she smiled—"he would have rather died than turn mulewhacker."

"The trail shapes a man, one way or the other," he said.

Spindles clucked steadily against thimbles in the rolling wheels. There would be plenty of teamsters in Santa Fe willing to return and get the other wagons out of the valley, but the girl wasn't thinking of that as she studied Brooke's hawk-like face, haggard now, hollows beneath his high cheek bones from the pain and hardship they had gone through.

"When your wound heals, David," she murmured, "I suppose you'll be going back to your Cheyennes."

He smiled faintly. "I've wandered a long time, and, after all, I'm really a white man. A white man should marry before he becomes a hermit of the Trail. I've always thought I'd want my wife to be a beautiful woman. And, Julie, those Cheyenne squaws don't hold a candle to you."

THE MAN WHO TAMED TOMBSTONE

I

He was probably the only man in Tombstone who hadn't run to see Kaye Lawrence arrive. He stood alone in the door of the Crystal Palace Saloon on the corner of Fifth and Allen. He seemed interested only in the deck of cards he shuffled through his thick fingers.

In Bisbee, they had told me of Odds Argyle who ran the Crystal Palace, and I wondered if this could be him. Then, still standing in the door of the Tombstone-Bisbee stage, I looked on over the shifting heads of the crowd to where the Dragoons thrust their purple crags out of the desert east from town, and I forgot Odds Argyle, and nostalgia cut me like a knife.

"Get down, greenhorn, and give us a gander at the lady."

The rest of the mob began shouting, and as soon as I jumped down, I felt the savage, unbridled violence of them, jamming me up against the coach, and I had trouble controlling the sudden desire to elbow them away from me. *Eddie Hammer,* I told myself, *take it easy*. Kaye Lawrence stood in the door of the coach now, and the men had forgotten me. Her dark hair was done up in a lustrous pile beneath the chic pink of her Parisian hat, and the green velour gown shimmered across the rich curve of her bosom. In all the rising dust and heat, I wondered how she could look so cool and regal, her red lips glistening a little over the shadowed line of gleaming white teeth her smile revealed. A last man clattered around the corner of Fifth and Fremont, calling to someone.

"What's up, Al, what's the ruckus?"

"It's the opery singer come to preform at the Bird Cage," answered a bearded miner. "She's purtier than Lillie Langtry."

I was jostled by a tall man in a black fustian and pin-striped trousers who pushed up to the battered Concord, bowing to Kaye like a courtier. "You seem to be without an escort, ma'am. May I assist you out of that atrocity Wells and Fargo have the temerity to call a stagecoach."

"The lady has an escort," I said, and could see how drunk he was.

He didn't seem to hear me. "Allow me to introduce myself, Miss Lawrence. Rhodes. Doc Rhodes. Your slave, Miss Lawrence."

I could begin to feel the restless shift around me, and I knew that sign in a crowd. "The greenhorn'll take care of the lady, Doc," one of them called sarcastically. "Didn't you hear?"

I tried to elbow Doc Rhodes aside and hold up my hand to Kaye. "Gentlemen, will you please make room for Miss Lawrence?"

They pushed in around me closer, and Doc

Rhodes reached up and pulled my arm down, and one of the mob shouted: "Ain't she a looker, and take a gander at that hat!" Then someone began singing a ribald ditty about Maisie's hat down on Allen Street, which, I gathered, was Tombstone's bawdy district. As Kaye's business manager, most of my job was handling the public, and I knew what a mistake it would be to let myself go with this crowd in such a mood.

"Let go my arm," I told Doc Rhodes, trying to keep my voice even. "Will you please step back for the lady?"

"Let go the greenhorn's arm, Doc," mocked the bearded miner.

"She ain't no lady," someone else shouted, "she's an actress!"

Maybe that did it. Or maybe Doc Rhodes tugging on my arm. I whirled suddenly and jammed my free forearm across his throat and shoved him against the crowd. They spread away from me, but Doc tripped on a cowhand's boots and fell on back into the miner and the miner staggered back and tripped across the high curb, and they both fell into the dusty street.

With the crowd laughing and roaring around him, Doc Rhodes got up with the solemn dignity of the inebriate, brushing his black satin lapels carefully with a long pale hand. Then he turned to me and I saw his eyes clearly for the first time. They were big and bloodshot behind heavy dissipated lids, and strangely soft. The men had stopped laughing suddenly, and, in the silence, Doc Rhodes's voice was as soft as his eyes and as deadly.

"Nobody knocks me down like that," he said, "drunk or sober. Would you care to apologize?"

"Not particularly," I said.

"Oh, God," called the miner, and the crowd spread with a sudden clatter of boots against the sidewalk, backing into doorways and out into the street, and Doc Rhodes and I were standing alone there facing each other.

"Then I consider that you have insulted me," said Rhodes, "and I demand satisfaction." He stepped out from the curb and slapped me in the face.

For just that moment I stood there with the sharp sting of his white palm on my cheek. Then, my own rage blinding me to anything else, I took a jerky step backward and grabbed beneath the left lapel of my coat.

"Hammer!"

It was Kaye's voice, cutting through my heat, cold and clear, and it stopped me and held me there with my hand gripping the spur trigger on the Remington-Rider in my shoulder harness. Doc Rhodes's long legs had bent into the kind of a crouch I knew well enough, and his hand was stiff above the black rubber grip of the Colt beneath his fustian. Slowly, I straightened, trembling a little with the effort it took to control myself now.

"You're drunk," I said. "Come back some time when you're sober." I didn't pull my hand free until I had turned clear around to help Kaye down.

She was soft on my arm, dragging it down a little deliberately with her weight, muttering in my ear: "Take it easy, Hammer. What's the matter with you? We've done a hundred towns and you've never let it get you like this. Tombstone's no different. A little wilder, maybe. No different."

Doc Rhodes hadn't moved from between us and the curb, and his elbow still held the tail of his coat off the Colt's black butt. "Does the lady usually pull her skirts out for you to hide behind this way?"

"You're in our way," I said carefully.

He swayed slightly with his liquor. "We haven't finished yet."

"I told you to come around when you're sober," I said. "I don't fight with drunks."

Rhodes flushed and started to say something, but Kaye turned one of her smiles up at him. "Please, Mister Rhodes. Have you so lost all your gentlemanly instincts as to carry on a common brawl in the street with a lady present?"

Perhaps it was the musical caress Kaye could put into her voice, or perhaps it was her stunning beauty. I had seen it affect men that way so many times before. The palpable tension left

Doc Rhodes's long body, and his face relaxed suddenly, and he was staring at her like a schoolboy with a crush. Suddenly he stepped back and bowed so deeply he almost fell on his face, and though he was under her spell, his voice still seemed faintly mocking.

"Truly, ma'am, I forgot myself. You are right. No gentleman would comport himself so abominably in the presence of a lady. My deepest apologies." But as we stepped onto the walk and moved by him, he straightened, and though he was still speaking to her, he was looking at me, with that soft deadliness back in his bloodshot eyes. "But you can tell your Mister Hammer that I will most certainly be around when I'm sober, I will be around very soon, when I'm sober."

Garrison Whitehall owned the Cosmopolitan Hotel, as well as the Bird Cage Theater where we were booked. He was a small bustling little man whose paunch filled his bed-of-flowers waistcoat the way a successful businessman's should, and whose toupee kept slipping back on his fat pate.

"I hope you'll find everything to your satisfaction, Mister Hammer. Sorry about what happened in the street, really sorry. Too bad you had to antagonize Doc Rhodes like that. He's probably the deadliest man in Tombstone. Drunk and gambling all the time and never paying his bills, but one of the deadliest." He waved his hand without bothering to connect his subjects. "And one thing I'm reluctant to broach. I said I'd have your full fee as soon as you arrived, but you see, the Chiricahua Kid . . ."

"The Chiricahua Kid?"

Maybe it was the sharpness of my voice that drew his eyebrows up in that surprise. "Yes. A bronco Apache. Uses red arrows. Murderer, bandit. Very bad. He disappeared from around here about fifteen years ago but he's come back just recently. And as I was saying, because of this Chiricahua Kid's activities, Tombstone has been veritably isolated from the rest of Cochise County, stage schedules all upset, telegraph wires cut, people afraid to come in or go out. And now the banker's agent from Bisbee is two days late, which creates an unfortunate situation. In the early days, the companies used to pay their miners at the source, with dust directly from the mine, but now they pay by check and you can understand what a drain the weekly draw of some twenty-five hundred miners would have on the bank. This is only a branch of Gibson's National here, and whenever there is an unusually heavy Saturday run, like last week, they depend on the banker's agent to supplement the drain with specie and coin from Bisbee."

"Yes?" I said.

"Yes," he said. "And now, as I say, the agent hasn't arrived yet, and Gibson's is unable to

71

meet the Saturday pay checks. You couldn't find this situation in any other town on the face of the earth, but here, where everything's crazy anyway"—he made that gesture with his hand—"in a mining center, mind you, the saloons and other places of entertainment depend mainly on the miners for their business. Now, with the miners temporarily insolvent, as it were, we'll have to extend them credit until we either get word from the company officials in Bisbee authorizing the paymasters to issue dust here, or until the banker's agent arrives. Naturally I was depending on the receipts of the Bird Cage to fill out the fee I agreed to pay you, but the only receipts I'll be getting now are chits, until the banker's agent . . ."

"All right," I said. "All right. Everything's fine, Mister Whitehall. We'll trust you until they do whatever's necessary to pay the miners. Now, it's been a hard trip and Miss Lawrence will need to rest before curtain time."

"I understand," he said, backing toward the door. "Believe me. And I'm sorry about Doc Rhodes, I really am. The deadliest man in Tombstone. Yes. The deadliest man."

I was still trembling a little with what had happened in the street, and I didn't know whether it was the anger yet in me or the reaction. I turned to the long mirror set in the door of the bedroom, straightening my black string tie until I could find more control. The glass reflected my face with its high cheek bones and broad facile mouth, a little twisted now, and black hair straight and thick as a horse's mane. I wasn't a tall man, but the shoulders of my suit weren't padded, and still the tailor had to cut them back wider than usual.

The room was done in a singularly atrocious Queen Anne manner, with buttoned plush of a sickening green hue for wall coverings, and brilliant-striped damask upholstering on the gilded sofa and Turkish ottoman. Reflected in the mirror, I could see Kaye's wry face as she looked around. She caught me watching her and laughed.

"When I settle down for good, Eddie Hammer," she said, "I'm going to have every room of my house done in Sheraton, with plain plaster walls."

I walked to the window without looking at her again, shoving aside the heavy Oriental portieres to look down on Fifth Street. Kaye moved in beside me, dropping the pretense suddenly.

"Thank you, Hammer," she said.

"I did it for you," I said. "I wouldn't have done it for anyone else."

"I know," she said. "And I don't think another man would have done it at all. It always takes more courage to back down than to go on, when you really want to go on. But Rhodes *was* drunk, Hammer, and there isn't any honor in meeting a drunk that way. I never saw you let it get out of hand before. Always the suave easy sophisticated Eddie Hammer, so completely the master of the situation that no one ever gets a chance to call your hand. What happened this time, Hammer? How did you let it get so far?"

I didn't answer; my glance was turned down Fifth toward the Dragoons. She reached up a cool forefinger and ran it down the hard line of my jaw, turning my face toward her until I had to meet her eyes, big and luminous and dark, and somehow fearful. "Is this it, Hammer?" she asked huskily.

"Is this what?"

"You looked at those Dragoon Mountains the same way when you got off the coach," she said. "I saw your face. Why, Hammer? You've been restless ever since we crossed the frontier. More than restlessness. A change. And now, down in the street, Hammer. I've never seen you show so much anger. The way you jumped back. Almost savage. I didn't think you were capable of that. I've seen you handle men so many times before . . . you've always been able to cope with whatever came up. But never like that. Never letting yourself go like that."

"He slapped my face," I said.

"No," she said and made me look at her again. "Something more, Hammer. Something that has to do with this change. I've always felt I didn't know you completely. You've been with me five years, Hammer. You've been my manager, my nursemaid, my confidant, my friend, always there, always responding to my moods so perfectly, yet I felt I never quite knew you. And I have a right to know you, Hammer. You kid around and play the game and never commit yourself, and I don't know how you feel about me, really. But you know how I feel about you and I have a right to know. What is it, Hammer?"

I patted her shoulder. "I think maybe it's the heat. You take a nap and you'll feel better this evening. I'll have the maid bring up a pitcher of milk and you take a big glass and have a nap."

Her eyes narrowed speculatively. "Is this it, Hammer?"

"You said that before. Is this what?"

"Tombstone," she said. "You never told me where you came from. You just showed up in New York playing marvelous piano at Timmie's Grille and you made me a business proposition and we've gone to the top on it and that's about all I know. Where's your family? Where do you come from? I saw the way you looked at the Dragoon Mountains. Is this it?"

I chuckled. "Who would want this squalid little hamlet for his home town? Anyway, how could it be? Tombstone wasn't founded till around Eighteen Seventy-Nine, the same year I was meeting you in Timmie's Grille. Now you have that nap, and I'll see you about seven for dinner."

I left Kaye with a strained look on her face and went down the hall to my suite. Always kidding around and playing the game and never committing myself? Sure, that's me, I thought bitterly, that's Eddie Hammer. A hundred times I'd wanted to tell her how I really felt about her, a million. But always there was that barrier between us. She had thought it was my natural reserve, and had tried to break through without knowing what she fought. But what good would it have done her to know, what good would it do for me to tell her? None. It would be the beginning of the end between us, that's all. She had sensed it from the first, as she said, and now, down in the street today, without recognizing it for what it was, she had seen it. . . .

I stopped with my hand on the gilt knob of my door, one step into the parlor. He sat deep in the wing chair by the ornate fireplace and his heavy fingers shouldn't have been so deft with the deck of cards he shuffled constantly. He was the man who had stood incuriously in front of the Crystal Palace when every other male in Tombstone was breaking his neck to see Kaye Lawrence.

"Odds Argyle?" I said.

He sat motionless except for his hands, not answering for a moment, still watching the cards he played with. His tremendous torso was foreshortened in the chair, and the development of his shoulders precluded any neck, his close-cropped bullet head rising directly from the gorilla slope of his upper back. His lips were thick with the mixed blood in him—mulatto, maybe, or Creole, or half-breed. His voice rustled through the room like the whisper of a woman's skirt.

"Yes," he said softly. "And you, I take it, are Mister Edward Hammer, Miss Lawrence's business manager. Italian?"

"I'm often taken for a foreigner," I told him.

"You're dark enough," he said. "Sit down, Nogales. Does Mister Hammer make you nervous?"

He was speaking to the black-haired Papago Indian with a dragging leg who had been moving incessantly about the room touching things with feathery fingers. Nogales didn't sit down; he didn't look at me either. But for a moment he was turned so I could see how he carried his big Remington six-gun stuck naked through his belt in the middle of his stomach.

"Funny," said Odds Argyle, still watching his cards. "Funny. You wouldn't expect these miners and cowhands to go for the high-brow entertainment. Dance-hall stuff and the girls down at Maisie's and a tin-can piano maybe, but not opera singers and concert stars."

"You make a mistake if you think they don't go

for it," I said. "We've been on tour six months and I've yet to see a house with an empty seat in it."

"No," said Odds Argyle, and a king appeared briefly in his fingers and disappeared. "No, I don't make a mistake. I know what a pull you city slickers have. Sit down, Nogales."

Nogales went on moving about the chamber, noiseless, in dirty bare feet, touching a Wedgwood vase on the mantel, passing his hand softly over the gleaming damask on the sofa back. Odds Argyle's cards kept up their constant fluttering sound. Neither of the men had looked at me yet and it was getting on my nerves.

"If you were wanting to meet Miss Lawrence," I said, "you'll have to wait till after the show tonight."

"If I had wanted to meet Miss Lawrence, I wouldn't have come to you," said Odds. "You're the business manager? Let's do business. How much would it cost, say, for your singer to get laryngitis, necessitating that you cancel your booking here?"

"That would mean forfeiting Whitehall's fee," I said.

"Of course," he said. "But say, if Miss Lawrence got sick, say you would get as much as Whitehall wanted, plus five thousand dollars. That's good odds. Sit down, Nogales."

"There are professional ethics involved here,"

I said, "which I have never sullied before. I think you've made a wrong bid."

"Or a low bid?" he said. An ace of spades slipped through his thick fingers. "Seven thousand five hundred?"

"You must have a pretty expensive reason to want Miss Lawrence out of town," I told him.

"Never mind the reason," he said. "Ten thousand?"

"It's getting toward suppertime," I said. "The first evening is usually a difficult one. I'd like to rest before the show."

"You force me to point out, Mister Hammer, that there are other considerations," said Odds Argyle. "Yes. I am never a man to make threats. I don't have to. But if the money doesn't touch a responsive chord in you, then there are other considerations."

"Tell Nogales not to move any farther down the wall," I said.

Odds Argyle's chuckle was sibilant. "Oh, Mister Hammer, you do me an injustice. I see you understand the other considerations, but not in a hotel room, please. So many people saw me come up . . . so many will see me leave. No, most certainly not in a hotel room. Sit down, Nogales."

"In the street, then?"

He hadn't looked at me yet and he shrugged his tremendous shoulders. "You sound so specific.

But we might as well use it for an example. Yes. The street, then. An amateur would deem it the obvious, dangerous, crude place. But really it's the safest, the subtlest. One has a hundred witnesses that it was purely self-defense. There are always methods to make it look that way, you know. There are more murderers walking around free today who did it that way than the ones who used a back alley. Or a hotel room."

"Doc Rhodes your man?" I asked.

"He frequents my establishment." Odds smiled, and his cards made a fluttering sound.

"That was your deal then?" I said. "Before you wasted your money, you thought you'd try it that way."

"Whatever Rhodes did out in the street was his own affair," said Odds. Then he slapped his cards together into their deck and, holding them with both hands, looked up.

I had been waiting for it, but still couldn't hide the shock of meeting his eyes. They were intensely, bitterly black and filled with a strange feline glow and it struck me that Garrison Whitehall made a mistake tabbing Doc Rhodes as the most dangerous man in Tombstone. Then I became aware that Nogales had at last looked at me too, and I felt myself stiffening imperceptibly against the door.

"However, Mister Hammer," said Argyle, "as I mentioned before, I don't have to make threats.

I see you realize what I'm driving at. There is a lady involved, and this is the wildest town west of the Missouri and almost anything can happen, any time. Won't you reconsider? Won't you reconsider for ten thousand dollars, plus Whitehall's original ante? That's good odds. Nobody would give you better."

"It's getting toward suppertime," I said.

Argyle's cards made a soft, fluttering sound in his hands. Nogales shifted his bare feet against the carpet. In that moment I could hear their breathing.

Then Odds Argyle rose without apparent effort and stood there, shorter than me by a head, probably twice as broad across the shoulders, flat-footed and spread-legged and perfectly balanced like a cat, waiting for Nogales to go out the door ahead of him. He stopped in front of me a moment, following the Papago, and studied his cards intently when he spoke.

"As I said," Odds murmured, not looking at me, "I don't have to make any threats. This is the wildest town west of the Missouri and almost anything can happen, any time."

II

The Bird Cage Theater was a long adobe building on the southwest corner of Sixth and Allen, its trio of fan-lighted doors topped by Romanesque arches of brick. Whitehall and Kaye and I stood in the wings of the small stage that evening, watching the shouting crowd of miners and cowhands fill the auditorium. It wasn't a large house and couldn't begin to accommodate all of Tombstone's miners, but the night shift was below ground now and there were enough seats to draw most of the trade away from the saloons on Allen Street.

There were seven boxes on each side of the auditorium, the first one on either side low enough to be level with the stage. The door of the near box on the right side was thrust open and a man wearing the marshal's star on his short gray coat came in and took a rickety chair. The overhead lights cast his square face into deep shadow from which his blue eyes gleamed as cold and humorless as the muzzles of the twin six-shooters poking the black toes of their holsters from beneath his coat.

Whitehall nodded greeting to him, muttering to me: "Marshal George Graham. Shows you how things stand in town. Ever since Tombstone was founded, almost, the city marshal and the county sheriff have been on opposite sides of the fence. Marshal Graham's crowd always sits in the boxes on this side, Sheriff Nevis and his bunch take the ones on the other side. Whatever Graham's faction applauds, Nevis's men immediately boo."

"That would seem to put the performers in a spot," observed Kaye.

Whitehall nodded, looking quickly to the other side. "There comes Sheriff Nevis now."

Sheriff Nevis was a man whose belly undoubtedly kept him too far away from the bar to get his foot on the rail and whose guns had too much silver plating on them and whose posterior overflowed the rickety seat into which he lowered it. Only one man followed him into the box. With most of the others in coats, he wore a blue serge vest, wrinkled up around his neck by the strain his great shoulders put on it. He sat down without looking at the stage, shuffling a deck of cards. Odds Argyle.

The boxes behind Nevis filled up with his deputies and cowhands. The miners and townsmen sitting around the small tables on the main floor began to beat their beer mugs on the planks and stamp their feet. Someone threw an empty bottle and broke one of the oil footlights. Marshal Graham stood up, cold blue eyes frowning on the shouting stamping crowd.

Sheriff Nevis stood up, his paunch overflowing the gilt railing.

"Bring out the gal!" shouted someone. "Let's see the show."

"Sit down, Marshal, and let the boys have their fun!" yelled Nevis. "Ain't every night they get to see a woman like this."

Marshal Graham's voice was chilly. "Sit down yourself, Nevis. Long as I wear the marshal's badge in this town, nobody throws bottles at a lady. Next man that does it gets thrown out."

Sheriff Nevis's crowd began to stamp and boo, and the men on the main floor added their catcalls and stamping to the din. Whitehall said something from the wings that was lost in the sound.

" 'Good-bye, Dolly Gray,' " I told Kaye, giving her a loud one, "and hit it!"

It was an old square grand, and I struck a dead G on the first bar, but I put my weight on the keys and it made enough noise to partly subdue the shouting. Then it was the rich fulness of the voice I knew so well, ringing out above the piano and all the other sounds and filling the little theater with the notes that had brought down houses from New York to San Francisco. She hadn't finished the verse of "Good-bye, Dolly Gray" before the men had stopped their noise and forgot their drinks and sat there enthralled, open-mouthed, bug-eyed, drinking it in. Perhaps it was their hunger for sight of a woman like this, illumed above them in the soft glow of the flickering oil lamps serving as footlights, the dark wine of her gown accentuating the alabaster of her shoulders, her black hair forming a lustrous frame around the pale oval of her face. Or perhaps music was something that could touch all men, red or brown or black or bad or good.

When she finished, Marshal Graham and his crowd stood up to clap and cheer, and the whole lower floor rose as one man, rocking the house with their applause, and Nevis and his crowd so forgot themselves as to join in wildly with the clapping. Only Odds Argyle remained seated, shuffling his cards. When the portly sheriff sat down again, Odds leaned forward to say something in his ear. Sheriff Nevis flushed, nodded angrily. I didn't like it.

The next number was "My Heart at Thy Sweet Voice" from *Samson and Delilah*, and Kaye could afford to do it softer and with more feeling now that she had their attention, and I made the mistake of losing myself in the music.

Mon Coeur s'ouver a to voix,
Comme s'ouvrent les fieurs. . . .

Then, through her voice and the piano, I began to hear the stirrings on Nevis's side, in the boxes behind him. One of his deputies began beating on the railing. A cowhand broke a bottle on the table with a loud crash.

"Sing it in English!" he shouted.

Marshal Graham stood up again, but the noise drowned his voice. Someone threw a bottle at the stage and it crashed into the footlights, breaking three of them on the right side.

"Nevis!" shouted Graham. "Take that man out!"

"Sing it in English!"

Aux bai-sera de l'auro re. . . .

"Give us 'Old Folks at Home.' "

Kaye could hardly be heard now, and Graham's orders didn't have any effect. The men on the main floor began to join in, shouting and stamping. Then a drunk in the rear box pulled a gun and began shooting at the overhead lights. Two cowhands in a nearer box hauled their iron and opened up at the stage. A footlight tinkled out; a slug skidded across the piano.

I didn't stand up to do it. I lifted my legs and swung them over the piano bench and had my Remington-Rider out of its shoulder harness by the time I was facing the audience. My three shots were the last ones.

In the silence that followed, the scrape of the drunk's chair sounded startlingly loud as he stood up, passing his hand across his head where his hat had been a moment before. One of the cowboys turned in his seat to look at his Stetson where it lay in the corner of his box, a bullet hole puckering its crown. The third man was looking at me with his mouth open a little, and he was bareheaded too.

"Just drop your guns over the railing, gentlemen," I said. "And let me warn you that the next time I won't confine my targets to your hats."

Their guns sounded heavy and metallic, hitting the floor below. I swung my legs back over the bench, laying my Remington-Rider on the square mahogany top above the keyboard.

"Miss Lawrence," I said, "will now sing '*Ah, Fors' E Lui*' from *La Traviata*."

Marshal George Graham came to my dressing room after the performance. Kaye had sung off and on from eight until two, providing the drawing card which kept the audience in the hall, drinking and eating and watching the other entertainment, and though the night shift had come in from the mines at twelve, there had been no more trouble. I was undoing my sweat-soaked string tie and saw the door open behind my back, and stiffened. Graham leaned against the frame, shoving aside his short gray coat to hitch his hands in the smooth black belts of his Colts.

"Never saw anybody handle a Tombstone crowd that way," he said. "But then I guess they

87

never saw a man handle a gun like that, either."

"I thought shooting men's hats off was one of your principal diversions here." I shrugged.

"Not like that," he said. "Not by a city slicker sitting down at the piano in his soup and fish. Sort of stopped them cold. Rather unfortunate for you, in a way. By muzzling Nevis's boys that way, you put your boot right down deep in the mud of this town's politics, and it won't be so easy to pull it out again. But maybe you tasted the bad beans before this evening. I saw Argyle and his Papago bad boy go into the Cosmopolitan this afternoon. Threaten you?"

Maybe my voice was mocking. "But, Marshal, Odds doesn't have to make threats, don't you know? He just put up a proposition. He didn't tell me why."

"Obvious enough," said Graham. "On the surface, at least. Every time Whitehall gets a famous star booked for the Bird Cage, all the other saloons along Allen Street might as well close their doors, for the business they do. I'll bet Odds's Crystal Palace didn't sell ten jiggers of rye tonight."

"Ah," I said. "The motive."

"Odds has more than one motive for wanting you out of town," Graham said. "You saw Odds in the box of our good Sheriff Nevis? It never has been clear whether Odds tells Nevis what to do, or Nevis tells Odds . . . but either way, they ride the same horse. Nevis got his appointment as sheriff through pressure the Allen Street bunch, headed by Odds, put on the county commissioners. A lot of Nevis's political strength lies in the weight the Allen Street bunch put behind him."

"And your strength?"

"There are still decent people left in Tombstone," said Graham coldly. "They form a bloc about as strong as Nevis and Odds and the Allen Street gamblers, and the clash between us has been coming a long time. Nevis's reappointment comes up in two weeks and he can't afford to lose one foot of ground before then. As I say, his strength lies with the Allen Street bunch . . . what they lose, he loses. How much do you suppose passes through the Crystal Palace on a heavy night?"

"No idea. Five thousand?"

"Four times that would be conservative. Multiply that by all the other saloons on Allen Street. The sum you get is rather breathtaking, and it's the sum Odds and his bunch stand to lose every night you play the Bird Cage."

"While we're discussing finances," I said, "this little upset in your monetary system seems rather fantastic."

"It is fantastic," said Graham. "Under ordinary circumstances or in an ordinary town it wouldn't be possible. The normal balance of cash and credit would take care of any emergency like this. But this isn't an ordinary town or ordinary circumstances. Two-thirds of the business houses in Tombstone are gambling halls, either owned or controlled by the Allen Street bunch, or with interests allied to them. They could cash the miner's checks a hundred times over, but why should they?

"The money would go right into Whitehall's pocket. The bank running short and the failure of the agent to arrive on time was the chance they might get once in a hundred years, coming right at the time it did. But by refusing to put their cash and credit into circulation, the Allen Street boys have upset the whole financial system of Tombstone. They hold all four aces, with Odds shuffling."

"Seems sort of a laborious way of going at it," I said. "Wouldn't it be simpler just to get rid of the Bird Cage?"

"They've tried," said Graham. "Nothing can be proved, of course, but that business tonight was started by a Nevis man. Their hoodlums have started riots and wrecked the theater before, or their machine tried to bring pressure on Whitehall. But the Bird Cage diverts enough business from Odds and his boys to keep them from gaining a monopoly on Allen Street which would give them veritable control of Tombstone and Cochise County to boot, so I put my weight behind Whitehall."

"Rather a delicate balance of power," I said.

"Which your presence here might easily upset," said Graham without humor. "The political influence of Odds and his bunch consists principally of their financial strength. Two more weeks of losing as much money to the Bird Cage as they did tonight would wipe out a lot of their influence and weaken Nevis in consequence."

"Whitehall told me he was taking chits for half the business he did tonight," I said.

"And when the agent from Bisbee arrives, the miners will cash their checks and make those chits good," said Graham. "No matter how you look at it, Hammer, you're the goat of this whole thing. They've been filling this powder barrel ever since Tombstone was founded, and you've lit it and you'll be sitting right on the lid when it blows up. Think of the woman."

"She's never backed out of an engagement," I said, "hell or high water. I couldn't drag her free of Tombstone with a six-hitch mule team."

Graham shrugged resignedly. "I'd hate to be standing in your Justins from now on, then."

"Hammer doesn't wear Justins, Marshal," said Doc Rhodes from the hallway. "Can't you see those perfectly useless flat heels on his shoes?"

Marshal Graham gave Rhodes a chilly glance and shoved by him without answering, his boots making a hard acrid sound down the hall. Rhodes moved in with a lithe ease surprising in such height. He stood several inches taller than I, hatless, his tawny hair worn long and brushed back over his ears *à-la* General Custer.

"You told me to come back when I was sober," he said.

The first evening is always a strain, and I was rather tired. "Oh, don't be a fool."

A flush darkened his pale, intelligent face. "Don't call me a fool, Hammer. You insulted me this morning. I told you I'd be back. I'm sober now and I'm here and the woman isn't around to pull her skirts in front of you."

"Oh," I said. "A gentleman of honor. I should think you'd want it out in the street where everybody could see you cleanse the stain off your illustrious escutcheon."

His voice trembled. "Do you think I care about them? It's me you insulted."

"I thought Odds liked his work done on the street," I said.

"Odds?"

"The insult is a very laudable motive," I told him, "but it's Odds, really, isn't it? Odds on the street this morning. Odds now."

He bent forward and one of his hands began to open and close, and his voice grew hoarse. "I'm not doing this for Odds or anybody else. I'm a drunkard and a tosspot and a bum, Hammer, and I know it. But nobody in Tombstone would have handed me what you did on the street this morning and gotten away with it, and they know it."

The sincerity in him suddenly struck me, and I took a step back because it didn't figure, somehow, in the way I had things pegged. "Isn't this rather small quarters?"

"The smaller the better," he almost whispered.

I shrugged, and began slipping out of my coat, looking for his weight. He wasn't as slender as he appeared, carrying shoulders that could mean something if he knew how to use them. He got out of his fustian and unbuckled his gun, and I folded my coat on the table and unbuckled my shoulder harness and wrapped the straps around the smooth holster. Then I straightened, and understood it well enough now to know how we would come.

Doc Rhodes threw himself at me without a word, expelling his breath in a savage gasp. I heard the scuffle of my own feet on the bare floor as I shifted behind one shoulder with my left out front. He took it full in his mouth and came on in and his greater weight crashed me back against the wall.

There was a clattering tinkle, and a shower of broken glass from the smashed mirror falling over the both of us. Shaking my head, I ducked beneath his flailing arms and jumped to the center of the room.

He whirled and threw himself at me again. This

time he had his own left out. I ducked under it and put one into his belly. While I was still down there, his right got through my guard somehow, and after the explosion of pain in my face, there was another blow on the back of my head and I realized I had hit the floor. With a strangled cry he threw himself on me and caught my long black hair and started beating my head against the boards.

"Damn you!"

I don't know whether I said it or he did. I brought my knee up between his legs and he let out a gasp of agony and quit beating my skull on the floor. When we had gained our feet, he was still doubled over from my knee. He kept his left out though, and that length of arm favored him for a while.

Blood was sticky on my face and hands and I couldn't see out of one eye and the sounds I made were more animal than human. Somebody was shouting at the door but I was as filled with it as Doc Rhodes now, and I hardly heard them. Rhodes got his head down beneath my guard and butted me in the stomach and the whole room shook as I struck the wall with his head still in my middle.

"Hammer!" someone shouted. It sounded like Kaye. "Stop it, you fools. Hammer!"

I kept him against me with his head in my belly, holding one hand on the back of his neck and hitting him in the face from below with my free fist. Every time I slugged, he jerked up, gasping. Finally he got a thumb in my good eye and I couldn't see for a moment and lost him. Then I realized I was on my knees against the wall. I tried to rise.

"I can't get up," I said. "Damn you, I can't get up."

Rhodes was sagging against the opposite wall, and he had to spit out some teeth before he panted: "Then I've beaten you. . . ."

"The hell," I said, and threw myself at him from my knees, hitting him in his belly. He came down hard on top of me. Hands were grabbing at us from somewhere but I fought free and rolled over and over with Rhodes until we brought up against the opposite wall. He lurched up from beneath, striking wildly. Still unable to rise, I caught him by the shoulder and twisted him sharply. The back of his neck was turned upward for that moment, and it was where I hit him. He collapsed. I lifted my hand again and could feel my smashed lips peel flat against my teeth.

"Hammer," screamed Kaye, grabbing at my fist, "stop, please!"

I didn't try to get loose of her grip, because Doc Rhodes hadn't moved from beneath me, and even through my blind haze of rage I could see how it was.

"Never mind," I said hoarsely. "It's finished."

III

It was about six the next morning when I dressed and went down for my cigar. Managing such a celebrity as Kaye Lawrence, a big part of my job consisted of dealing with her public, and in the larger cities this morning hour was often the only time during the whole day in which I could be alone. I had hurt my hands in the fight with Rhodes, and the left one was so sore I could hardly light the match. Then I turned down Fifth, sucking in the chill morning air almost greedily, my shoes making a loose hollow clatter in the deserted silence. I hadn't gone far when the walk shook to someone else's boots. He came toward me, calling something. The slatted doors of the Oriental Bar creaked open and slapped shut behind a swamper, who came out still carrying his pail and mop. He set them down suddenly and kicked the pail over in turning to follow the first man, and the dirty brown water ran out on the planks and dripped through the cracks.

There were other men running north across the street now, and with a strange prickling excitement raising in me, I followed them. A stage stood in front of the Wells-Fargo office at Fifth and Fremont. There were only three horses in the team, two flanking the tongue and one leading them in a single trace and reins. Marshal Graham and one of Sheriff Nevis's deputies were working over something on the high seat, hiding it from view, and the driver stood on the sidewalk in the midst of a crowd, holding a bloody bandanna to his face.

"I left Bisbee for Tombstone last Friday," he was saying. "They hit me south of Lewis Springs. The team stampeded and I got thrown. Unconscious all night, I guess. Came to on Saturday morning and trailed the coach into the hills. They'd left it there, cutting loose the team and running it off. I don't need to tell you what the banker's agent for Gibson looked like. I buried him there and started toward Tombstone on foot. Late that afternoon I come across three of the team where they'd stopped to rest in a draw south of Tombstone. I took 'em back to the coach and rigged up a harness out of the traces and got started finally about ten last night. I couldn't get the shotgun guard off. I had to ride all the way in with him like that."

He waved his arm to where Nevis's deputy had dropped off the box seat, revealing what he and the marshal had been working on. The guard had been sitting upright in the seat, pinned to the back by six or seven arrows, any one of which would have sufficed. The heads had been buried so deeply into the wood behind the man that it had been necessary to pull his body away from the back of the seat and cut the arrows off behind him before he was freed. There were little lines of strain around Graham's set mouth as he sliced the last shaft and caught the body as it slumped forward. He reached around in front and pulled the arrows out one by one, holding them by their feathered ends. Then he allowed some of the crowd to lift the corpse off, and dropped down himself, looking at the arrows.

"The Chiricahua Kid?" said Nevis.

"I don't know," said Graham, rubbing his jaw. "I don't know. The Kid disappeared fifteen years back, Nevis. In Eighteen Seventy? Yeah, Eighteen Seventy. And before he disappeared, he never was any road agent. He was only fighting for his people, like Geronimo was in his earlier days. The Chiricahua Kid never hit a stage line before his first disappearance. . . ."

"Don't be a fool!" flamed Nevis pompously. "Who else ever used all red arrows? You saw how far they were driven in. Through the man and through the wood behind. You know any other Indian around here capable of handling a short bow like that?"

"No," said Graham. "Still . . ."

"Chiricahua Kid or not," said Garrison Whitehall, who had come from the Cosmopolitan in a striped dressing gown, "you'd better find whoever's using those red arrows before your reappointment comes before the commissioners,

Nevis, or they'll have a new man behind your star. That's the second stage in two weeks. And those Orejo ranchers last month."

Sheriff Nevis flushed, then he turned and heaved himself onto the sidewalk and stamped off toward the Crystal Palace. The crowd had begun to fade and I moved over to Whitehall.

"That's why the banker's agent was late," said Whitehall, waving his hand distractedly, "and there goes the miners' pay. They said the Chiricahua Kid got a hundred thousand or so in specie the agent was carrying."

"This is insane," I said. "In a town as rich as this, you'd think something could be done. How about all the gold you pull out of the mine every day?"

Whitehall shook his head. "We don't handle the crude stuff here . . . the refineries and stamping mills are in Fairbank and the bullion is shipped direct to Bisbee from there. As far as the dust goes, our wires have been cut . . . the Chiricahua Kid, no doubt . . . and we can't get anything through to Bisbee, and the paymasters here won't issue any dust without authorization from the officials in Bisbee. That's the Allen Street bunch again. They have strings on half the men in Tombstone, and half the mines . . . and when the paymasters refuse to move, they're speaking under pressure from Odds and the gambling crowd. It's become more than just getting the miners paid or not getting them paid, Hammer, don't you see? It's the final test between the two factions here in Tombstone, and your presence here forms the crux of the whole thing and the Allen Street faction is willing to upset Tombstone's whole economy to get you out. If the miners get paid and the economy is normalized before you leave, I cash in and the Allen Street faction loses its shirts for the two weeks you're booked here. They'll be in the red when Nevis's reappointment comes up, and the influence their money gave them will be gone. Without that influence behind him, Nevis will be out . . . and without Nevis to stand between them and Marshal Graham's party, the gamblers on Allen Street will be through."

"And if the town's economy isn't stabilized?"

"I'm the loser," shrugged Whitehall. "Which is what Odds and his boys are working toward. They know what a blow to me this business about the banker's agent is. I expected to cash in all the IOU's and chits I've been accepting when he arrived. I extended myself further than I should and I haven't been able to meet my own bills without any cash receipts coming in. Half the men I owe are under the influence of Odds and his crowd, and the Allen Street bunch will start putting pressure on them now and I'll be closed up. It's just a vicious circle. Under ordinary circumstances an established business like the Bird Cage could run several months on credit, but now, with Odds and his faction blocking every normal avenue of cash or credit, I'm about washed up."

"You'll open tonight?"

"Maybe for the last time." He nodded dismally. Then he shook his head. "We're talking about how it affects me, but the Bird Cage isn't the prime factor in this, you know. It's your presence here that moved the Allen Streeters to perpetrate this colossal absurdity. They're only trying to close the Bird Cage to get you and Miss Lawrence out. Be careful, Hammer. It isn't over yet."

He moved away, shaking his head and muttering irritably to himself. A pair of Wells-Fargo clerks had carried the guard's body into the office, and the only man left near the stage was the doctor, a red-faced little man with pince-nez glasses on his bulbous nose and a neat white goatee. He waved absently after the clerks.

"Can't do much there, can I?" he said. "I hear you had a little trouble last night, though. Your face all that got hurt?"

"Hands a little sore."

He took one and his gently probing fingers drew a gasp of pain from me. He looked up, still holding my hand.

"A *little* sore?" he said. "I should think so. You've broken just about every metacarpal in it."

· · ·

Kaye saw the splint when I came in, and the rich color left her cheeks because she knew what it meant well enough.

"Sorry," I said. "I should have thought of you. There's a point, however, in a thing like that, when a man quits thinking at all."

"I know," she said, and came close enough to disturb me with her perfume. "It's all right, Hammer. So I've lost my accompanist, so all right. You needed a rest anyway. We'll refund what money Whitehall's given us and maybe your hand will be healed enough to play again for our Tucson booking. It isn't that worrying me, though. It's the fact that you did quit thinking. I saw your face last night, Hammer. You were too far gone to remember, but I saw your face while you were fighting Rhodes. It frightened me. I never saw you like that before. You were always so reserved and self-controlled, such a master of any situation. In New York, you wouldn't have let yourself go like that. You would have considered the possibility that a fight might hurt your hands and you would have handled it some other way. What's gotten into you, Hammer? You're so changed."

I turned away sharply, going to the window. She didn't follow me; she moved around the room restlessly, finally began to make small talk.

"Reading the Tombstone *Epitaph* today. The

102

editor was quite upset about this financial crisis. Said the people were beginning to feel the pinch. At first it was just the big operators but now even the small money is getting tight. He was lacerating the paymaster for not putting the dust into circulation. It seems the logical way of easing the situation. I couldn't even get a ten dollar bill changed today. . . ."

Someone knocked on the door, and I heard the rustle of her skirts toward it. Doc Rhodes came in.

"Heard about your hand, Hammer," he said. "You won't be able to play tonight?"

"Tonight or any other night, in Tombstone," I said. "But what does it matter? Whitehall won't be able to keep his doors open much longer anyway, and he couldn't pay us even if I could play. One way or the other it would have been the finish."

"And the Allen Street bunch have gained their point," said Rhodes. "You'd like to stay?"

"It will be the first booking we had to cancel in three years," said Kaye sadly. "Professional pride you know. Sort of gets in your blood. If it wasn't for Hammer's hand, I guess we'd stay until Whitehall had to close, whether he paid us or not. I've gotten to like the fat little man, toupee or no toupee. It seems a shame he has to go down under the gamblers this way, without a chance."

"I used to play," said Rhodes.

I turned for the first time from the window, trying to keep the anger out of my voice. "What are you talking about? Can't you let it be? You fixed it so we're through here. That's what you wanted, wasn't it, you and Odds? What's the idea of this?"

"I told you last night I didn't have anything to do with Odds," he said. "The idea of this is that I used to play the piano, and if you want to stay, I'll try again."

"You can make that offer," I said, "after last night?"

"I'm not making the offer to you, Hammer," he said, and he was looking at Kaye.

We tried it out after lunch in the empty theater. Doc Rhodes *had* played. His crescendos were a little ragged and he had to cover a lot of sloppy treble work with his bass chords, but he must have had class at one time and it still showed. The house was packed by 8:30, with people even standing on the sidewalk outside to catch some of the music. I found Whitehall in the wings, fussing with his toupee.

"You'll stay tonight, Mister Hammer," he said nervously. "I know Doc Rhodes will do all right on the piano if you say so, but you won't leave, will you?"

"I hadn't thought of it. Why?"

He waved a harried hand toward the crowd.

"They haven't forgotten what you did last night. As long as you're in sight, they won't cause any trouble."

I was surprised how soon the noise stopped when I went out and held up my hands for silence and announced the first number. Rhodes was a little shaky at first, but Kaye turned part way around so she could meet his eyes as she sang, and he seemed to gain confidence from it. I remembered how she used to look at me that way.

An usher appeared in Marshal Graham's box while Kaye was doing a Stephen Foster medley, whispering something into the marshal's ear.

Marshal Graham frowned, gave Whitehall the nod. Whitehall moved to the box and bent forward to hear what Graham said, then Graham rose, cast a look across to Nevis's box, and left. Whitehall came back, shaking his head.

"Oh, why did I ever get into this business. All I wanted was a nice quiet neighborhood theater. Then I had to get the bright idea of booking Lillie Langtry on her tour through the West. It drew such a big crowd I had to expand the house. Now look. I'm not a theater manager. I'm just maintaining the battle ground for the private war between Marshal Graham's party and the Allen Street bunch. If I smile at Graham, Sheriff Nevis is liable to give Odds the nod, and the hoodlums from the Crystal Palace go to work on my chandeliers. If I look at Nevis, Marshal Graham might get it into his head to close me up for serving liquor after hours. If I hire good people, I'm bucking Odds Argyle . . . if I don't, I go broke. Why did I get into it, Hammer?"

"Graham?" I said.

"Oh." Whitehall made a vague motion with his hand. "Some trouble up on Fitch Street. He had to go, you know. His duty. Left word he'd be back as soon as possible."

"Fitch is way up at the other end of town, isn't it?" I said.

An usher tapped me on the shoulder. "The Wells Fargo man is out back, sir. Something about your passage to Tucson."

"But I have tickets," I said. "Tell him later."

"He says it's urgent. Something about cancelling the runs until this Chiricahua Kid is cleaned out. No drivers will take the coach or something."

"But we're booked in Tucson," I said. "We have to leave the Sunday after this one."

I looked at Kaye and nodded my head out back. She smiled an answer, still singing. I left Whitehall, muttering it would be only for a minute. The back hall was dark and I left the inner door open so I could see the stage from the outer portal, which led onto an alley. My shoes made a hollow sound down the passage. A man drew his dark shadow at the opening ahead.

"What's this about my passage?"

"We can't assure you passage," he said, stepping back into the alley, "on account of this Chiricahua Kid business. . . ."

His voice was muffled, and it was automatic for me to take a step through the door toward him to hear clearly what he said. Then I realized the Wells Fargo clerk hadn't been that big.

There was a scuffling sound from both sides and they were on me. One, two, ten—I'll never know. But what happened inside me occurred all in that instant while I was going down beneath them. In the theater behind, I caught the sound of a shot and the first yells, and knew why Marshal Graham had been drawn to Fitch Street and why I had been pulled out here—and suddenly I was swept with a rage that shook me more violently than the weight of their bodies slamming me against the ground. It was the same savage, primitive lust of battle that had gripped me in the fight of Doc Rhodes, blotting out all the sophistication and suavity and culture of those years with Kaye, unleashing every tameless, pristine animal instinct that had always lain beneath.

A blow struck the back of my head, driving my face into the bitter earth. Mouth filled with dirt, I convulsed beneath them like something erupting from the ground and heard my own ravening scream of utter, frenzied rage.

I grabbed an upraised arm and pulled the man down hard on top of me before he could strike, jamming my knee upward.

"Damn . . . ," he gasped, and collapsed on me. I hooked him around the neck and slugged him in the face and caught his gun and twisted it from his hand. Then I was on my knees, pistol-whipping at a second man, seeing him reel away and carry a third with him. Their very numbers were against them. Unable to shoot for fear of hitting one another, they milled around me, getting in each other's way. I took a blow in the mouth and, spitting out blood, threw myself against them toward the stage door, my own screams drowning out the other sound, slashing and firing with the gun.

"My God," shouted someone, "he's loco, he's loco!"

I hit blindly at a face and felt the flesh pulp beneath my blow and threw myself over the man as he fell away from me. Someone caught my coat. I kicked a man out of my way and slipped out of the arms at the same time, still going forward, forced to drop the gun so my hands would slide through the sleeves. I left two of them jammed in the doorway holding my coat and had my own Remington-Rider out by the time I reached the auditorium, thanking God it had been my left hand that was broken.

The place was swarming with shouting, cursing,

yelling men. A bunch of miners had pulled down a chandelier, and it made a glittering splash of broken glass in the middle of the fighting mob on the main floor. A cowboy from the lower floor threw himself into the rear box on Nevis's side, his weight carrying one of Nevis's deputies against the rail. The thin wood splintered and collapsed, and both struggling men fell into the seething crowd below.

Nevis wasn't in the first box, nor Odds. A bouncer from the Crystal Palace was climbing over the smashed footlights, followed by six or seven toughs from the other saloons. Doc Rhodes stood with his long legs spread on the edge of the stage, and a barfly already lay groaning at his feet, and one of the toughs reeled back from his clubbed Colt. Kaye stood right behind him holding a bottle by the neck for whoever wanted it first. Rhodes kept trying to push her back but she wouldn't move. Then he caught sight of me.

"Get her out, Hammer. I'll hold them off here. Get her out back!" He had turned around far enough by then to see me fully, and he trailed off with his mouth still open, a wide shocked look entering his eyes.

My shout sounded hoarse. "They're out back too, and coming in."

He was still staring at me that way, and it seemed an effort for him to speak. "We can't just stand here."

"We're going out the front!" I shouted, and caught Kaye around the waist and swept her toward the boxes along the side nearest to us. A drunk gambler was climbing over the railing onto the stage, and he grabbed for a gun and I shot him and he fell on his face with his feet still hooked over the gilt rail. Through the din I heard someone screaming like a crazed Apache and suddenly realized it was me.

I swung Kaye bodily over the railing and she was looking at me the same way Doc had, her eyes wide and shocked, and filled with a faint, growing horror.

"Hammer," she said unbelievingly, and put her hand up to her mouth. "Hammer . . ."

All the boxes opened onto a narrow hall which ran down between them and the side wall, leading to a stairway which opened onto the main floor. One of Nevis's deputies lurched from this passage through the door of the first box, levering at a Winchester. I vaulted the rail and swung Kaye around behind me, and my Remington-Rider made a dull boom over the noise. The deputy fell across one of the rickety chairs, smashing it with his weight.

From the height of the box I caught sight of the close-packed, deliberate little group of men standing at the three front doors, and then saw Nogales among them, Odds Argyle's Papago bad boy, and I realized what was happening.

The men by the door were all bouncers or barmen or gamblers belonging to the Crystal Palace and the Oriental Bar and they blocked the exit completely. Their intent was patent: they meant to keep the fighting crowd of miners and cowhands and townsmen inside the Bird Cage until it had turned the building to a shambles. Three screaming, kicking, cursing miners and a pair of high-heeled cowhands surged toward the door in their mass struggle. Nogales stepped out, pistol-whipping one of the miners across the face, slashing at a cowhand. A pair of bouncers followed him up with short clubs they used in the saloons. The trio forced the miners and cowboys back until they were caught up in the main battle again and had forgotten about trying to get outside where there was more room to fight. Then Nogales and his men moved back to block the door.

Doc Rhodes came jumping over the rail of the box, firing backward at the men who had swarmed onto the stage as soon as we had left it. I went through the door into the passageway first, stumbling over a body in the narrow darkness before reaching the stairs. Another deputy with a Winchester was coming up the stairs, and his first bullet made a hollow sound striking the wall behind me.

With thought of Kaye back there, I couldn't quit firing until my own gun was empty. I stopped long enough by the deputy's huddled body at the foot of the stairs to scoop up his Winchester, and I hit the main floor with the .30-30 clubbed. I went into a pair of yelling miners first and struck one hard enough to knock his chin out of his beard, and jammed the butt of the gun into the second one's thick belly. A cowhand loomed up and I hauled the gun back to swing, feeling my lips peel across my teeth in a snarl. A strange, terrified look crossed his face and he threw himself backward before I could hit him. I heaved myself bodily against the struggling press of men, hacking viciously with the clubbed rifle.

I chopped at a pale face and felt the dull shock of flesh and bone smashed beneath the hard oak of the gun's stock and saw a man hauling his short gun and I hit him across the chest with a backward swing that smashed him back against a pair of drunk townsmen and all three fell in a writhing heap. I jumped over their flailing arms and legs, driving a struggling group of miners ahead of me with my berserk screams ringing out over their shouts.

There was something about a rifle wielded like that which no crowd could stand up to for long, and I saw what was happening. I had driven them back until their press was surging against the Allen Street men blocking the front door, and Nogales was fighting a desperate, losing battle to hold the frenzied crowd inside.

Doc Rhodes lurched up beside me. He could wield his Colt with lethal effect at the end of his long arm, and the added fury of his charge beside me broke the ranks in front of us, and the crowd was no longer solid there and I realized they must have finally broken through Nogales. I saw him then, the Papago with the dragging foot. With his men scattered and the breach made, he no longer had any reason to stay at the door, and he had a reason to come through the crowd toward me that way with no expression on his dark face. It didn't need any expression to tell me his intent.

A frock-coated gambler got in my way with his derringer, and I hit him across the face and felt the splintering shock clear to my shoulders, and when I raised the Winchester again, the stock was gone from it.

"Look out, Hammer!"

Doc shouted it, because Nogales had broken through the last bunch of struggling men and his gun boomed from the hip. I felt something hit my side, and spun with the blow. Off balance, I threw myself forward with Nogales's second shot whipping by my head, and struck wildly at his gun hand with the barrel of the Winchester. He screamed with the pain and his Colt made a sharp, hard sound hitting the floor and when I struck again it was at his twisted face and I stumbled across his body before he had completely fallen beneath me.

I don't remember the rest clearly. Stumbling into the thinning crowd and hacking blindly at the bobbing faces with the broken barrel of the .30-30. Whitehall spinning from somewhere out of the haze and holding his toupee up in the air like a trophy of victory, shouting at me.

"Hammer, you've done it, you've driven them out, you've saved the Bird Cage, Hammer!"

Other faces appearing from the fetid surge of the mob, and hands, and legs, and screams, and my own hoarse, animal sounds. Then someone grabbing at me from behind, and Kaye's voice.

"Hammer, stop, stop! It's all over. You can't chase them clear down Allen Street. Are you crazy? Hammer, stop!"

Kaye was shaken up a little, but nothing else, and after giving her something to quiet the nerves, the doctor tended to my wound, which wasn't as bad as all the blood would seem to indicate, and then he and Doc Rhodes left. I couldn't remember much of the fight, but now I noticed Kaye watching me intently, a sort of puzzled fright in her big dark eyes.

"What got into you?" she said hesitantly. "The same way you were when you fought with Doc Rhodes the other night. It scares me, Hammer. You were like a raving maniac. No wonder they couldn't stand up to you. The whole crowd. When you came running in from the back, Hammer. Your face. Like a madman. An animal. What was it?"

I took a deep, shuddering breath, beginning to feel the full pain of my wound and my bruises. "What would you want me to do, give them Brahms's 'Cradle Song'?"

"Don't be like that." She shook her head sickly. "I can't understand it. You were always so cool and deliberate, so completely in control of all your emotions."

I said: "The time hasn't come for that kind of explanation, so let's forget it. There are pleasanter subjects. Your Doc Rhodes, for instance, was doing rather brilliantly at the piano before that business started. You seem to work well together . . . he'd be a good accompanist for you."

"*My* Doc Rhodes?"

"You like him a lot," I said.

She put her hand up to stroke my shoulder, not meeting my eyes. "Hammer. Eddie . . ."

"Never mind," I said. "I don't blame you. He's a very charming fellow when he wants to be. Cultured, smooth, amusing. Got a lot of good qualities. And he hasn't touched a drop of red-eye since that first day you arrived. Given time, your influence would undoubtedly regenerate him completely."

Her voice was sharp. "Don't talk like that."

I took her by the shoulders. "I mean it, Kaye. If you like Doc Rhodes, that's fine. Maybe I've misjudged him . . . maybe he isn't in this with

Odds. It certainly didn't look like he was tonight. If he isn't, then that fight he and I had doesn't count."

She looked up at me. "You really mean it, don't you? You aren't being sarcastic. You don't even sound jealous."

"Was I ever?"

"You never showed it," she murmured. "But you know there was never anybody else, Eddie."

"Did you ever consider," I said, "that your feeling about me might not be the real thing, might just be the result of our intimate association over such a long period of time, sort of a habit, like drinking old-fashioneds even though you really don't like them?"

"Oh, no!" Her voice had risen. "No, Hammer. That isn't so. You never told me how you felt, but you know how I feel. Don't ever say that."

"Why not?" I said. "Are you afraid to face it? I saw the way you looked at Doc Rhodes tonight. If there's any doubt in you, look at it. Then look at Doc again."

"Eddie . . ."

It had been a long time since I'd done this, but I couldn't help how I felt about her, even if I'd always hidden it, and I tilted her chin up and kissed her. She was breathing hard when it was over, and she pulled away to look up in my face.

"You never did it like that before, Hammer," she said. "It was almost like . . . good-bye."

IV

I didn't wake until about nine the next morning, so stiff and sore I could hardly roll out of the bed. I soaked in a hot tub for half an hour, with a cigar, and took my time shaving. Kaye's room was empty and I shut her door softly after standing there a moment remembering the countless breakfasts we had eaten together like that. Whitehall met me in the lobby.

"Miss Lawrence up yet?"

"She had a breakfast date with Rhodes," I said. "You look happy for a man with a wrecked theater."

"I've just been down looking at the Bird Cage," he said. "The Allen Street bunch thought they'd smash the place? They've got another think coming. They didn't count on you, did they?"

"But they did," I said. "They sucked me out just like they sucked Marshal Graham. That wasn't any Wells Fargo man at the back door."

"I know, I know," he said, "but you got back in, didn't you, and stopped the riot before the Allen Street bunch held them in there long enough to wreck the house. You're a terror when you get going, Hammer. So quiet and gentlemanly and unassuming ordinarily. Wouldn't suspect you had that wild streak in you. I wish you would stay here permanently. Most of the lights were smashed, and the furniture, but I'm having new fixtures installed this morning and hauling out some of the old tables I stored away when we redecorated for Lillie Langtry."

"Where did you get the credit for the fixtures?" I said. "Why go to that trouble? You said you were through."

"On the contrary," he chortled. "Why do you think the Nevis faction perpetrated that riot last night?"

"I wondered," I said. "They already had you sewed up, and the Bird Cage would have closed anyway. Why go to the trouble of wrecking it?"

"Because their little plan to upset Tombstone's economy is all washed up," he said. "Word came last night, just before the show. I didn't hear about it until this morning, but they heard at the time, and that riot was a last desperate attempt to finish things. Wells Fargo runs a spur line from the stamping mills at Fairbank directly to Bisbee, and one of their stages passed our coach the night of the hold-up . . . it must've been just after the Kid had cut loose the team and left it, and before the driver had come back to it. The Fairbank stage carried the news on to Bisbee. A rider hit Tombstone, coming in from Bisbee last night, just before curtain time, and he brought word that the bank is sending another agent with the money and a big enough military escort to stop every

118

Apache in Arizona. They should arrive tomorrow sometime."

"I suppose Nevis knows?"

"He knew it last night." Whitehall grinned. "That's the reason for the riot. And he knows you prevented the mob from wrecking the theater. He knows you've blocked them again, Hammer."

Graham came into the hotel, his gray Stetson not quite hiding the bandage on his head. " 'Morning, gentlemen. I hear our Mister Hammer stopped the show last night."

"You should have seen him," chuckled Whitehall.

"I guess they thought they had it all set up," said Graham. "Nothing can be proved, of course . . . nothing ever can. Odds and Nevis were out of the Bird Cage before anything started, I take it. That trouble on Fitch Street was to suck me out. They put a Colt's butt to my head on a dark spot on Fifth Street. I had my suspicions when I left the theater, but I had to go, you understand. I walk just as narrow a trail as Nevis. One misstep and I'm off. Refusing to go last night would have given the Allen Streeters a wedge to separate me from my marshal's star. Claiming I was neglecting my duty or something. And neglect of duty would stick in the city council's craw."

"You and the city council, and Nevis and the county commissioners," smiled Whitehall.

119

"County commissioners is right," said Graham. "The word you put in got some action. The county board told Nevis he'd either better clear up this Chiricahua Kid business or be looking for another job when his reappointment comes up in two weeks. Nevis put a pair of his Papago trackers on the trail the Kid made getting away from the stagecoach job last Friday. One of the Papagos came in last night with news that they'd struck hot tracks and followed them into the Dragoons. The tracks led on through the Dragoons to the Chiricahuas, but the Papagos wouldn't go any farther without the sheriff."

"I wouldn't go on either," said Whitehall. "Patagon and his Apaches are holed up there in the Chiricahuas somewhere."

"Patagon?"

"Means Big Foot," Marshal Graham told me. "The Army nailed Cochise a long time ago in Stronghold Cañon, and trapped Geronimo in the Sierra Madres last September, and this Patagon is about the only bronco Apache left. More than one white man has wandered too near the Chiricahuas and never come back. The Allen Street bunch tried to keep Nevis from going, but this time it's the Kid or his job. The Sheriff left this morning about three o'clock. Fat and pompous and crooked, you still got to hand him credit. Mighty few men would go in there after the Kid."

Doc Rhodes came in through the door, a smile

on his battered face. "Well, compatriots, is Miss Lawrence up yet?"

"I thought you had a breakfast date with her?"

"I did. Ten o'clock. I'm on the dot."

It was a long moment before I spoke. "She wasn't in her room."

Whitehall tugged at his toupee. "You don't think . . . you don't . . ."

I was past thinking. It was like the night before. I didn't hear the hard apprehensive rattle my shoes made on the front steps, nor feel the man I shoved aside, nor know whether Rhodes and the others were following me as I ran down Fifth. A lone barman was in the Crystal Palace, leaning a disconsolate elbow on his polished mahogany, and the place still reeked of stale tobacco and whiskey from the night before. He took his elbow off the bar and looked surprised and that was all I saw before I ran by him. There was a balcony over the bar with stairs leading up at either end and three doors lining the wall. I shook the stairs going up, and that was what Nogales must have heard. The Papago came out of the last door, dragging his leg.

"Odds's room?" I called.

He was in front of the middle door before I had reached the top of the stairs, and I could see the weal across his face I had made with the rifle the night before. "He ain't here, Hammer. You can't go in."

"Don't try and stop me, Nogales!" I shouted.

"I'll stop you," he said, and went for his gun.

After it was over, I stepped over his body and shoved the middle door open, my Remington-Rider still in my hand. It was a sumptuous office with a heavy Chippendale desk in the middle and oils of nudes on the wainscoted walls and a faint odor hanging in the air. None of Odds's dancing girls would use perfume that expensive. Kaye's Barbanche scent!

"He shot Nogales. Hammer. He murdered Nogales!"

It was the barman shouting it, and it whirled me. He stood in the hall on the other side of Nogales's body, with a couple of miners and a swamper, and behind him was Rhodes and the marshal, and through them I could see more men coming in the saloon. I backed across the room.

"She's been here, damn you," I said. "That's her perfume. You had her here."

"Who?" said the barkeep. "What you talking about? You can't . . ."

"Stay right there," I said, and shoved up the window, still holding the gun on them. "Hear that, Doc? They had her here."

It was a long drop to the alley below and I turned my ankle. Limping, I headed toward the runway between the Crystal Palace and the stables next door, which led me out onto Fifth. Men were already running from the saloon. I knocked the reins of a pinto from the first rack I came to, and swung aboard.

"There he is!" yelled a miner. "Hammer!" He began shooting.

I swung the pinto out into the street and had it in a gallop by the time I passed the Cosmopolitan, heading out of town. I could hear horses behind me, and began reloading my gun, putting my shoes into the pinto, and wishing they had spurs on them. But I had known where I was heading and had picked the best horse on that hitch rack for the job, as hurried as I had been. The pinto was a tough hairy little brute with chunky hocks that meant enough speed in the get-away, and a bulging curve to his windpipe that meant plenty of wind for the endurance I would need on the longer run, the kind of a horse an Indian would like.

I passed the sage flats east of town with pursuit still in sight, but had shaken all except one man by the time I reached the foothills. He had a big rangy gelding and there was something about his seat in the saddle that caught at me. I pulled in the pinto and turned with my gun up.

"That was a fool thing to do," called Doc Rhodes, "burning down Nogales."

I slowed down and let him bring up with me. "He pulled on me."

"That won't stand. Somebody ditched Nogales's gun and the Allen Street bunch are already claiming you did it in cold blood. They'll have the town whipped up to lynch you on sight. How can you do anything for Kaye now?"

"They had her in that room," I said. "I'm after Nevis. If I get my hands on him, he'll tell me where she is, believe me."

"I do," he said. "But why Nevis?"

"Because we don't know where Odds is," I said. "And Nevis is in with Odds, isn't he? The sheriff went after the Chiricahua Kid? That sounded all right at first. How does it sound now? Did it ever strike you how convenient it was for the Allen Street faction that the Chiricahua Kid should stop that specific stage. It prevented the agent from reaching Tombstone and would have meant Whitehall was through if the Fairbank coach hadn't happened to pass the Tombstone-Bisbee stage just after the hold-up. Has the Kid's work ever coincided with the Allen Street bunch's business before?"

"Come to think of it," said Rhodes, "yes. The sole support of the school at Tombstone is derived from an operating tax on the saloons. Last month, Odds and his gang tried to repeal the tax. The decent people in Marshal Graham's party opposed the measure. The biggest part of their bloc was formed by ranchers in the Orejo Basin. The Kid raided the Orejo, and by the time he was through, the ranchers were too. A rancher without a spread is as useless as a saddle without a cinch. Their opposition ceased and Odds put through the repeal and the school is no more."

"Marshal Graham seemed to doubt it was the Kid."

"He was right about the Chiricahua Kid never doing that kind of work before his disappearance," said Rhodes. "Only time you found those red arrows in a white man then was when the white man gave some good provocation. But nobody else ever used them, and who could shoot a bow like that?"

"Ever see the shoulders on Odds Argyle?"

"You mean he's the Kid?" said Doc.

"No," I said. "Odds Argyle isn't the Kid."

We found Sheriff Nevis in the Dragoons. Taking the old Cochise Trail through these mountains, we had topped the crest of the last ridge and were dropping down toward the Chiricahua Basin when my horse shied at something beside the trail I wouldn't have spotted. I had my gun out by the time I was on the ground, and found him in the timber a ways.

The arrow through his leg must have struck him first, knocking him back against the tree with its terrific force, where he had fallen to a sitting position, getting the second shaft through his belly then. It was driven in so deeply through him and into the pine trunk that only the last red feathers showed against the darker red of congealed blood covering his paunch. He didn't recognize me at first.

"The double-crosser," he babbled. "I didn't know he was doing that. All along he was doing that. I didn't know I was trailing *him* when I went after the Chiricahua Kid. He got my Papago trackers. See 'em?" Then Nevis recognized me. "By God, Hammer!"

"Who were you trailing, Nevis?" I said. "Who's double-crossing you?"

Sheriff Nevis didn't have long to go and he was delirious, I guess. "Leave it alone, damn you. I been pulling at it all day, trying to get loose. Turned my guts to hamburger. What you doing here? Damned double-crosser. Leave it alone. How'd you find me?"

I quit trying to free the arrow. "Graham told me your Papagos had stuck hot tracks in the Dragoons. They were following the Chiricahua Kid and he would have taken the old Cochise Trail through these hills because that's the way the Indians always take."

"Only an old-timer'd know the Cochise. You're a greenhorn. You, Doc?"

"I didn't know the Cochise existed," said Doc. "This is Hammer's."

"How'd you know, Hammer?" gasped Nevis faintly. "Who are you?"

"Yes," said the man who had stepped from

the trees on the slope above, "who are you, Hammer?"

Odds Argyle carried a hickory short bow in one hand and a bunch of long red arrows, and it suddenly struck me how easily he could have passed for an Indian if his hair were longer. I hadn't done anything with my gun because of the others behind Odds. The old one had a turkey-red bandanna about his coal-black hair, and the hip-high Apache *botas* folded over until they reached only his knees, providing a double-thickness of buckskin to protect his shins from the brush. The Winchester he held in the crook of one elbow wasn't pointed at me, but enough of the others were, held by the half-dozen young bucks standing behind him.

"*Hola*, Patagon," I said. "It's a long time since the Cochise Stronghold."

His feet made a small surprised sound, shifting in the pine needles. "No *belin'ka*," he said, using the ancient name for white man, "would know about the Stronghold."

"The Chiricahua Kid?" I asked, waving my hand at Odds.

Patagon nodded. "He returned to us five years ago."

"He's been dealing from two decks, then," said Doc Rhodes. "In Tombstone he's known as Odds Argyle."

"Of course," said Patagon. "That was the way

we've been doing it ever since he returned. How do you think we've managed to remain free out here? Whenever General Miles sends out another expedition against us, the Kid, living in Tombstone as Odds Argyle, warns us in time. He can keep us supplied with ammunition and even rustled beef when the hunting is bad. He has helped us raid the Orejo and the Pinta."

"How do you know he's the Kid?" I said. "Did you recognize him when he came back?"

"The Chiricahua Kid was only twenty when he left our people in Eighteen Seventy," said Patagon. "He returned to us a man of thirty. There were few of us left who had known him as a boy and it would be hard to recognize anyone after so long, especially when he had changed from a boy to a man. But as soon as he shot the bow, we knew him. None of our warriors could equal the Kid on the bow."

"Did you ask him where Cochise is buried?"

"Why should I?" said the old Apache.

"If he's the Chiricahua Kid, he would know, wouldn't he?" I asked. "You and the Kid are the only ones left who know where Cochise is buried, Patagon. You accepted Odds Argyle as the Kid merely because he could shoot the bow? You accepted him and did whatever he said because he was the Chiricahua Kid? When he wanted you to rob a stagecoach or raid a ranch or ambush a sheriff, you did. You're getting old, Patagon.

Twenty years ago you wouldn't have accepted him so easily. Did you need his help that badly? Why don't you ask him now the things he should know? Ask him why the Apaches never gather *beyotas* in Stronghold Cañon, Patagon."

Patagon hesitated, looking at me strangely, then turned slowly to Odds Argyle. A doubt darkened his old eyes, and the other Apaches were looking at Odds, too. Odds made a vicious gesture with his bow.

"Don't listen to this loco . . ."

"Can't you tell him, Odds?" I said. "Go ahead. The acorns are ripe in Stronghold Cañon but the Apaches never touch them there. The Chiricahua Kid knows why, and Patagon. Tell him, Odds."

Odds's voice was a hoarse whisper. "Damn you, Hammer."

"Why," said Patagon, "don't the Apaches gather *beyotas* in Stronghold?"

Odds opened his mouth to speak, then closed it again. I waited a moment longer, until it was clear that he wouldn't answer.

"The Apaches never gather acorns in Stronghold Cañon because it is the spirit land of Cochise," I said. "They buried him there, and the Chiricahua Kid and Patagon and others who are now dead rode their horses from one end of the cañon to the other all day long so that all signs of his grave would be lost forever."

"Only the Kid and I would know that," said

Patagon, looking at Odds. "You don't?" Then it must have struck him, because he turned toward me suddenly. "Then, you are . . ."

"The Chiricahua Kid," I said.

V

Odds's breath made a small, hissing sound in the silence. Then, taking that moment while they still stood in shocked surprise, he jumped at me with an explosive grunt. It caught me off guard and his solid weight carried me back against Doc, and the three of us fell to the ground. While I was still going down on top of Rhodes, I felt Odds's thick fingers around the hand I held my gun in. The terrible strength of that momentary grip drew a gasp of pain from me, and when he let go and grabbed my gun, my numb fingers released it without resistance. He jumped on over Doc and me. I tried to turn over on Doc and grab Odds's feet; he kicked me in the face and was on past. The Indians had recovered from their surprise and were jerking at their Winchester levers. Odds was turned far enough around by the time he reached my pinto and the Remington-Rider boomed in his hands with the first shot and one of the young bucks fell forward on his face. Odds swung aboard the pinto, emptying my gun at the Indians in a swift series of shots that set them jumping for cover while they tried to pick him off the horse with snap shots. By the time I got up off Doc, Argyle already had the pinto going down through the trees.

Patagon shouted something and the Apaches scattered into the trees above the glade where their horses must have been. Doc had caught his mare and was already turning her after Argyle. I started to run downslope after them, then stopped, realizing how useless that would be on foot. Argyle was already gone and Doc was disappearing into the aspens at the foot of the slope. There was a crashing to my right and the Indians made their brief, flitting shadows through the pines, heading their mustangs in a breakneck gallop after Doc and Odds. I made a jerky move their way, then stopped again. It was suddenly very silent in the glade. With a biting frustrated anger shaking me, I heard Sheriff Nevis groan, and moved to him, cursing myself for letting Odds surprise me like that.

"My horse," said Nevis faintly. "Staked on that juniper down the Cochise about a quarter mile. Left it there when we spotted the Kid and came in after him."

He slumped over the arrow holding him to the tree. Dead.

It was a big Morgan mare and it had been there a long time and it was fretting with thirst. I swung aboard it, forcing the animal toward the ridge top above me; it took me fifteen precious minutes to find a naked place where the timber didn't obstruct my view. Then I could see down the east slope into the Chiricahua Basin.

The riders were barely perceptible below me, but I could see what had happened. Canny old Patagon had cut in between Odds and Tombstone with his Apaches, forcing Odds to turn away from the direction he would have taken back to town. He was headed across the basin now, not willing to meet them on the open flats. He was heading straight into the Chiricahuas.

I slid the Morgan through the talus to timberline and bent low in the big Porter saddle on down through the belt of white pine and juniper and finally aspen, into the open sage flats of the basin, the harsh, familiar crags of the Chiricahuas looming nearer and nearer as I drove the animal through the choking dust. They must have caught up with Odds in the foot slopes. It was where I found the first Apache. He lay in a bed of ocotillo, with the red arrow protruding from between his shoulder blades, gripping his own short bow in one hand. It struck me for the first time how near the end my people must be. In the old days I had been the only one using a bow; the others riding with Cochise or Geronimo had all carried the newest repeating rifles and latest Colts and scorned the weapons of their fathers. But now it was like Graham had said. Cochise had been caught by the Army in Stronghold so many years ago, and Geronimo had been trapped in the Sierra Madres last September, and now it was only Patagon left, with his handful of ragged warriors, making their last stand, reduced to using whatever weapons they could get their hands on. The bow was this Apache's only arm, and I had to take it or nothing. In my rage at being such a fool and my frenzy to get Nevis's horse, I had completely forgotten I was without a gun. I worked the buck's dead fingers from around his handful of arrows. Why not, though? It was fitting, somehow. If I met Odds, it was what he would use.

The Apaches called it *Say Yahduset*, which meant Point of Rocks, and they believed the voices of the dead could be heard here on a moonless night. It was a weird, haunted place, somewhere deep in the Chiricahuas, formed by succeeding eons of eruption and erosion and inundation, its red and yellow pillars of sandstone thrusting up from pock-marked buttes which were surrounded by huge masses of granite that spread their fantastic shapes across the black fields of lava and into gleaming knife-edged draws of pure schist. I came upon the pinto below the first spectral slope of the *Say Yahduset*; it was down and dying from more than one gunshot wound. Halfway up the slope were the Apaches' mustangs where Patagon and his men had left them, because a mounted man topping that first ridge would have skylighted himself to whoever was beyond. I left the Morgan among them, and took off my coat so the tails wouldn't get in my way, and removed my shirt because the white cloth was a dead giveaway on a bare slope.

My skin lacked the ruddy color outdoors would give it, but the racial darkness was still there. I found Doc's horse near the top, standing hipshot and jaded in the meager shade of a huge black boulder. They were all farther in, then, stalking Odds, and I squirmed over the ridge with a film of sweat already bathing my body from the heat of the sun, oiling my muscles and giving my movements a smooth felinity they hadn't possessed in fifteen years. It was the old game now, and that was how long since I'd played it. I found a spot in the soft dirt where the Apaches had gathered, evidently for a pow-wow, and then separated to spread a net around Odds. I trailed one of them down the slope into the bottom of a valley and turned down the valley a ways through the fantastic formations of granite and lava to where a *sere motte* of dry cottonwoods threw their disconsolate shadows. Climbing the opposite slope, I found the second dead Apache. He sprawled back against a boulder where the force of the arrow had carried him. I was still trying to tell how long ago he had been shot by how thickly the blood was congealed in his wound, when the dribble of shale came down from the ridge above me. I whirled, and Odds had just topped the lava uplift and was as surprised as I.

"Hammer!" he cried, and he had his arrow already notched, and I saw the surprise in his face as he jumped down.

I didn't make the mistake of trying to get my arrow notched. In that last moment, I threw myself back into the fissure below the boulder and heard the twang of his gut and felt the arrow drive past my head and strike the rock behind me. I had my arrow in the string before I hit the bottom of the narrow fissure and I lay there, stunned and bruised by the fall, waiting. His voice came rustling down to me, soft as the whisper of a woman's dress.

"So you're the Chiricahua Kid?" he said.

He was smart enough; he knew what he would have gotten if he let his excitement bring him in after me. But he also must have known how little time he had, with Patagon and Doc out there somewhere.

"I thought you and Nevis were on the same horse?" I said, and tried to place him when he spoke.

"In Tombstone we were," said Odds Argyle, and there was a faint scratching sound beneath his voice that might have been made by his body moving across the shale. "But there were things

I needed which Nevis couldn't do for me, or wouldn't."

"Like the stagecoach?" I said.

Odds's voice was sibilant. "Yes. Nevis didn't have the stomach for the dirty jobs like that which had to be done once in a while to protect our interests. I couldn't let that banker's agent reach Tombstone and get the miners paid off, could I? If I'd used ordinary triggermen on any business that benefitted me as obviously as that stagecoach operation, the Graham faction would have pointed the finger my way. They couldn't blame me for what the Chiricahua Kid did, though, could they? Whenever those red arrows showed up in someone's belly, nobody ever connected me with it. I started it about five years ago. My father was a Yaqui and maybe I got my talent on the bow from him. And maybe Patagon needed help bad enough he didn't ask too many questions when I, as the Chiricahua Kid, showed up in his camp with my proposition."

"Kaye?" I said.

He chuckled thinly. "Only as a last resort, Hammer, only as a last resort. All our other attempts to get rid of you had failed. You wouldn't accept my offer that first day, and you botched the riot we tried to start by shooting off those hats. When we got word that another banker's agent was coming through with a military escort, I knew Patagon's Apaches couldn't help me

136

stop that stage like we did the first one, so we started to wreck the Bird Cage again. Only you broke that up, too. Nevis was against taking the woman, but we had to do something to get you out of there before the second banker's agent arrived. Nevis was afraid of what you'd do if we took Kaye. You had him buffaloed and he was trying to back out of the deal."

"That's why you shot him?"

The small scraping sound came again. "No. I still needed him to stand between me and the Graham bunch in Tombstone. But the damned fool had to come out after the Chiricahua Kid. I pulled that stage robbery last Friday and sent the agent's specie with Patagon, who brought it back through the Dragoons by the Cochise Trail. I was back in Tombstone the same day. When the driver came in Sunday with the coach and the dead shotgun rider, Nevis put his Papagos to tracking me and Patagon away from the spot where we'd left the stage."

"He didn't know you were the Kid."

"Of course not," said Odds. "I told him to drop it, but the commissioners were on his tail. We got Kaye Lawrence about two-thirty Monday morning. It couldn't have been much later that the sheriff's Papago hit Tombstone with news that they'd cut the tracks made Friday from the stage hold-up, and followed them into the Dragoons. I made the mistake of taking Miss

Lawrence through the Dragoons on the Cochise, because that's the way we always went. Nevis wasn't actually following me when he caught up. He was on those tracks Patagon and I had made Friday. I guess he thought he'd caught the Kid red-handed. Well, maybe he had, but not the way he figured. He came in shooting. What else could I do?"

He had covered his movements by his voice and I hadn't been able to follow him because the wind coming down off the ridge carried the sound the wrong way, and now he was where he wanted to be, and it was coming. I opened my mouth, and couldn't hear anything. I quit breathing, and that didn't help. I began to remember the shotgun guard, pinned to his seat by arrows driven so deep the stage driver hadn't been able to get him off alone. And Nevis, held to that pine all morning with the single shaft. No wonder the Apaches had accepted Odds as the Kid. Few men had that power on the bow. It was those shoulders.

But there was more than power involved. It was an axiom on the frontier that a good bowman could loose six arrows so fast that the sixth would be in the air before the first had struck its mark. The first arrow had struck Nevis in the leg, and he had the time to stagger back and fall down in a sitting position against the tree before the second one had pinned him to the trunk. That long an interval between the two arrows might indicate that Odds had depended too heavily on his natural power, neglecting to develop his speed in proportion. It was the only thing I could count on.

The wind whined down the slope and scattered talus sibilantly across the slickrock, and it was the only sound. My hand was sticky with sweat around the *Bois d' arc* of the bow I held. The lip of the fissure began to undulate with purple heat waves.

"All right, Hammer!"

His broad bulk loomed suddenly from behind the lifting granite and his gut made its sharp twang. I threw myself forward so my momentum would keep me from being carried backward by the terrific drive of his arrow, and with the shaft making its dull thwucking sound in my shoulder and twisting me halfway around, I had my gut back to my ear, and jerked squarely to the front again, and still stumbling forward, let the gut snap.

"All right, Odds," I shouted, and then shouted again, every time an arrow left my bow, "all right, all right, all right!"

Going ahead in a staggering run, I had my fourth shaft out before the first had hit him. The surprise crossed his face as he saw my skill for the first time, and then the anger as he realized he could never get his second arrow notched, and the pain as my first bolt struck him in his thick chest.

He staggered backward with its force, trying vainly to put his arrow on his gut. My second one drove home and he took another stumbling step backward, dropping his bow and his handful of arrows. My third one made its dull fleshy sound going in, and his hands were clawing at the three shafts as he fell backward, and the fourth one went home before he had fallen.

I sat down because the pain of the one through my shoulder nauseated me.

I don't know how much later they came. Doc Rhodes was first, and he began cutting the shaft free with his Barlow knife. Then Patagon. The old Apache nudged Odds's body with his foot, looking for a long moment at those four shafts buried so close together in Odds's chest. Then he turned to me.

"The woman is in our camp, Kid," he said.

The teepees were much like the dome-shaped Navajo hogans, the frame of cottonwood branches thatched with mud and leaves. A handful of ragged squaws in tattered red blankets and a dozen fierce, ragged warriors with bandoleers of Winchester shells crossed on their naked brown chests stood around us while the shaman brought Kaye from the medicine lodge. Her face was stained with tears, the rich wine of her gown smudged and torn.

"Someone came to my rooms last night,

Hammer, after you left. I didn't recognize him as Odds's man. He told me you'd gone back to the Bird Cage and gotten hurt badly. I didn't stop to think, Hammer. More of them were waiting at the theater and they took me to Argyle's office and held me there till they brought the horses around the back way to that alley." She stopped, turning her wet eyes up to me. "They told me. Patagon. The Chiricahua Kid? You said you hadn't come from Tombstone."

"I told you Tombstone wasn't my home town," I said. "I left here, before Tombstone was founded. These mountains are my home, Kaye, the Dragoons, the Chiricahuas. I rode with Geronimo, until he quit merely defending his land and people and took to raiding and plundering and killing on any excuse, or none. That wasn't right. It's honorable enough for a man to defend his country and I'm not ashamed of anything I did. But I couldn't take it Geronimo's way. I was twenty when I broke away and drifted East. At Saint Louis, I got a job in the Rocky Mountain House, working in the taproom, and ran into an old broken-down music teacher entertaining there. Edward Forsythe Hammer. He gave me more than his name. He took me under his wing and found out I picked up things fast. Taught me English and discovered I had a talent on the piano. I guess he was mainly responsible for my becoming the Eddie Hammer you knew, Kaye. It was ten years from the time I left here till I met you in New York. A man can get a lot of polish in that long a time, if he works at it, or has a talent."

"Why didn't you let me know?" she said huskily.

"I couldn't bring myself to do that," I said. "I knew our separation would date from the day I told you who I really was. No matter how much you fought it or tried to ignore it, it would have always stood between us . . . it was what formed the gulf between us anyway, Kaye, even without my telling you. And merely telling you wouldn't have done any good, Kaye. You would have laughed and told me I was a fool to think it could stand between us. A person has to see it to understand.

"Haven't you seen it now? When I had the fight with Doc, and the night of the riot at the Bird Cage. You saw it and you were horrified. As soon as we hit the frontier, all those old things began to boil up in me, Kaye, the primitive things, the animal things. I thought I could blot them out with education and culture and civilization, but I was wrong. I was never happy in New York . . . I was always lonely and apart and inhibited with trying to act civilized. I couldn't live in your world and you couldn't live in mine, Kaye. You don't want a savage for your husband, a man who goes crazy like that when he gets into trouble, you don't want half-breeds for children. . . ."

"No, Hammer," she said desperately. "How can that change my feeling for you, how can anything?"

"What is your feeling?" I said. "You thought it was love, and when you met Doc and began to have your doubts, you were afraid to face them. Five years is a long time to be together, Kaye, and you form ties and habits you're afraid to break when the time comes. Admit it to yourself, Kaye. I saw the way you looked at Doc when you were working. He's your kind. Get away from me and break all the old ties and you'll see what you felt for me was just the result of being together so long. You sensed our difference from the first, Kaye, and you were fighting it all the time. You won't have to fight Doc. He's your kind. . . ."

She began to cry hopelessly, and I looked across the dark perfume of her hair to Doc, and he understood. They helped her on a horse, unresisting now, and she turned in the saddle to look at me for the last time.

"That kiss in the Cosmopolitan last night," she said. "You knew then. It *was* good-bye."

I nodded without speaking. The horses lifted a dead gray dust downslope out of the camp. Patagon moved in close beside me.

"We let Odds Argyle lead us because we thought he was the Chiricahua Kid," he said, "and he led us the wrong way, the way Geronimo had. Now we have found the real Kid, and you said you left because you couldn't do it that way. How *would* you do it?"

I motioned back into the Chiricahuas. "There are valleys back there which the white man will never see while we are alive. We can return to the old ways."

"I've been trying to tell them that." Patagon nodded. "I think the younger bucks will take it from the Chiricahua Kid when they wouldn't from the old man. Yes, the old ways." He looked after Kaye and Doc. "You were right about the gulf between you and the woman. It would have been like trying to make the sun and the moon rise at the same time. Perhaps you were right, too, about her not really loving you. But how did you feel toward her, Kid? You never said."

"No," I told him huskily. "I never said."

BULLETS AND BULLWHIPS

I

Blackie Barr halted uncertainly at the rear end of the wagon train parked beside the Reno stage route, just outside the sprawling Kansas cow town of Caldwell. He held his dark head down, looking defensively from beneath heavy black brows, his eyes dull and lifeless. Where there should have been strength in the thick shoulders swelling out his checked flannel shirt, there was only a defeated sag. He fumbled a bottle from the canvas war sack under his arm and uncorked it with his teeth. But the whiskey was flat and tasteless. Even that had ceased to help him, now.

Blackie cast a dull glance at the twenty big Murphy wagons bulking ahead—Pop Trevers's train. Old whang-hide Pop Trevers was the only man who had stuck beside Barr in his defeat and shame.

Just a week ago, Pop had found Blackie in Dodge City's Alamo Saloon and had dragged him almost bodily to the Trevers's freight office. It was a small musty room, that office, with a rawhide-seated chair that groaned when Pop tilted back in it and propped his worn Justins on the scarred oaken desk.

Trevers had stuck gnarled thumbs in the

armholes of his blue serge vest and run knowing old eyes over Barr.

"Likker don't sit so good with you, Blackie. Three years now, ain't it? Been hittin' the bottle all that time?"

Blackie's puffy face had paled. Yes, three years—three years since his wagon train had burned at Raton Pass and five men had died in the fire. He'd been wagon boss for Southwestern Freighting. They had held an investigation, an inquest, and Blackie Barr had been discharged, damned, and dishonored, blackballed from every freight outfit west of the Missouri.

Blackie had bent forward suddenly, gripping the desk till his knuckles showed white, pouring out all his pain and bitterness to the man who'd been his father, friend, and teacher all in one.

"Sure I've been hittin' the bottle all that time, Pop. What'd you have done? I'm an outcast from the only world I knew. Men I thought were my friends shun me now, or laugh at me, or kick me because I'm down. I can't get a job in any freight outfit . . . not even in their stinkin' cavvy yards. And do you think the lives of those five men that burned in the fire sit easy on my soul? I'm just as much their murderer as if I'd shot 'em to death!"

"Take it easy, son," Pop had said softly. "I know how it is. I only wish you'd come to me sooner, but I guess you was ashamed. You whacked bulls for me a long time afore the Santa Fe Trail bug bit you, and you switched to Southwestern Freightin'. I just can't believe Blackie Barr'd be careless enough to let his whole train burn down. I always thought there was somethin' fishy about the whole thing."

Pop Trevers stopped for a moment, a strange softness entering his gaze. "Whether you was to blame or not, son, you shouldn't let it keep you down on your knees in the mud this-away. You got the guts to fight back up to the top where you belong. I got a gov'ment contract to ship supplies from Caldwell to Keeche Agency in Oklahoma Territory. I already hired me a wagon boss, but if you want a boost toward the top, Blackie, that's a bull team waitin' for you down at Caldwell."

For a moment, their eyes had met. Two years ago, the old man's offer might have given Blackie hope, but not now. Yet he knew it would break Pop's heart to have him refuse.

The faint bawl of the bull team came to Barr now as he took a last pull at the Monongahela whiskey and stuffed the bottle back into his war sack. He stepped off the road toward the wagons, gripping the coiled bullwhip in his fist until swelled and knotted muscles rippled through his hairy forearm, muscles that came from years of handling that heavy, twenty-foot blacksnake— once the most famous whip east of Santa Fe.

Rounding the tall Murphy wagon, Barr saw the crowd of bullwhackers gathered there, hidden from the road. They shifted, allowing a paunchy man to waddle through. A battered black soft-brim hat was mashed down on his triple-chinned face, almost covering the sly little eyes, set deep in fat cheeks. He wore a pair of black-handled Colts strapped across his gross belly and thonged down around thick, blue-jeaned thighs.

"Well, well," he chuckled, "if it ain't Blackie Barr. I heard ol' Pop Trevers hired yuh in Dodge. Be the first time yuh whacked a team since Raton, won't it, Blackie?"

Barr's voice was brittle. "Yes, Raines, since Raton. Which wagon's mine?"

The other grinned affably and for a moment Blackie forgot to watch those sly eyes. "Yuh sound different, somehow, Blackie. Whar's the ol' roarin', cussin', fightin' king of the trail I used to know?" His words merged into the chuckle that followed. The wagon boss turned to the men. "I guess you know most of the boys. And I guess they know . . . you."

Blackie half turned, for the first time realizing what an ugly-looking bunch of cutthroats they were. There was big Rob Davis, towering over all the others in buckskin breeches and hickory jacket. He'd been booted out of the Overland for whipping a team to death. Beside him was Steve Moore who had none of the thick-chested, heavy-bearded look of an honest bullwhacker. His face was narrow, sallow, and there was something snake-like in his glittering eyes. It was said that the six notches in the stock of his blacksnake were for men he'd killed with it.

Blackie shifted his war sack uneasily. "Where's my wagon?"

"Why, I reckon the last one in line is yours," said Raines.

Blackie started to skirt the crowd, but big stupid Rob Davis wouldn't let it go at that. He stepped heavily in front of Barr, a bucolic look to his thick-lipped face.

"How is it they hired you, Blackie?" he said. "I thought you was blackballed out of every company this side of Santa Fe."

Barr's head sunk a little into the weary slope of his shoulders. "I don't wanna talk about it, Davis."

"But I do," said Davis stolidly. " 'Bout Raton, for instance. Was you really dumb enough to corral your wagons too close to the fire, with no water in their kegs?"

A harsh edge entered Blackie's voice. "Damn it! I said I'd rather not talk about it!"

Suddenly Davis grabbed Blackie by his shirt front, pulling him forward until their faces were but an inch apart. There was a crushing strength in the thick arm holding Barr and he was helpless for a moment.

"Your wagon-bossing days is over, Blackie," snarled Davis. "You can't swear at me that-away."

With a violent shove, he straightened his arm, heaving Blackie backward. He fell, twisting sidewise, dropping whip and war sack. He hit hard, pain jarring through him.

As Blackie rose, shaking his head groggily, he sensed the new, waiting tension that gripped the crowd. Steve Moore was leaning forward with an evil smile. Raines had something malignant behind his bland smile. The others had moved in, watching Barr narrowly.

Blackie realized there was more behind this than Rob Davis's sullen hostility. The big man had deliberately baited him. It was their way of finding out if the ugly stories drifting down the bull-whack trail about Blackie Barr were true.

Well, they were true, weren't they? Three years ago Blackie Barr would have mauled Davis into the ground—all two hundred and ten pounds of him—and he would have laughed in doing it. Now all he could do was stand there with his head lowering defensively, nothing inside him but a hollow defeat.

Raines gave Barr plenty of time, then he chuckled. "Now, Rob, you shouldn't've done that. Blackie's had a hard time and he just ain't up to your hoss play."

Blackie bent to pick up his war sack and whip.

The men drew together, turning their backs deliberately on him—they'd found out what they wanted to know. As Blackie straightened, the wagon boss waddled over and clapped him on the back.

"Yuh won't hold no grudge, will yuh, Blackie?" he said. "After all, Rob is just a big impulsive kid." That seemed to amuse him and he chuckled until his paunch quivered against crossed gun belts. "Yeah, just a great big impulsive kid."

Blackie shrugged the pudgy hand off with a feeling of revulsion, moving heavily toward his high-sided Murphy wagon. He gave it an indifferent glance, then looked closer, frowning. The oak side boards were warped and split, the iron tires loose on the wheels, bound carelessly into place with buffalo tug. Even the oxen were poor, spavined, flea-bit. This didn't look like the kind of outfit Pop Trevers would have.

The sound of boots in the shortgrass turned him. Rita Trevers had come from between lead wagon and trailer, hitched tongue to axle. For a moment she stood there without speaking, disappointment in her big dark eyes.

Pop Trevers's daughter had been a long-legged pig-tailed kid when Blackie left the old man's outfit to see Santa Fe via Southwestern Freighting. She was a woman now, with lustrous brown hair and that generous Trevers width to her mouth. She wore a linsey shirt and a man's blue jeans tucked into yellow cowhide half boots. Her voice was strained when she spoke.

"I saw what happened out there with Rob Davis, Blackie. In the old days you would've come close to killing a man for that."

Blackie's face flushed dull red and his eyes fell. He didn't even try to alibi. What was the use? What disgrace, shame and liquor had done to him was all too apparent.

"I was glad, at first, when I heard you were coming," she said in a low tone. "I didn't think you'd sunk as low as they said, didn't believe all the horrid things I heard about you. I thought you'd still be man enough to help me."

"Help you?" Blackie asked dully. "What's the matter?"

"You saw for yourself. The wagons, the teams . . . it's the rottenest outfit on the trail. Something's wrong, Blackie, and I'm worried. I counted so much on your help. Then, when I saw you back down from Davis and those men . . ."

She stopped, a strange pleading in her tone, her face pale. It was a long, painful moment for Blackie, standing there with his eyes unable to meet hers, his lips a thin bitter line.

Then Raines's voice rolled back from the lead wagon, raising the familiar trail call: "Al-l-l set!"

His cry was echoed and re-echoed by each whacker, followed by a volley of crackling whips and the "hep, gee, haw" that drew a flood of memories from Blackie Barr. The old, nameless thrill ran through him as he tossed his war sack into the wagon and shook out the coils of his twenty-foot whip, laying the long tapered lash out in front of him.

Blackie gripped the twelve-inch stock, waiting for the braided leather wrapping to become moist with sweat from his palm. Then with a sudden practiced ease, he brought his arm back, keeping the elbow well away from his side. The lash whined backward past his head. Almost with the same motion, he reversed his arm, swiveling his wrist. The whole swift movement was deceptively easy, but the bullwhip snarled forward again like unleashed lightning, and the sudden sharp crack of its snapper above the yoked oxen had the thunderous sound of a .50-caliber Sharps.

The patient beasts lurched forward. The huge center chain dragged off the ground with a clanking of thick, iron links, and the big Murphy began to roll, its squeaking rumble sweet music in Blackie Barr's ears.

II

They made eight miles that day, not hurrying the oxen at the start, allowing them to settle into the trail. It was a long train—twenty wagons, each with three pairs of yoked oxen straining up front, and a trailer hitched behind. And beside every team, a bullwhacker walked, cussing his animals when they slowed. That cussing was the proud badge of a real whacker; it took a certain genius. It had been said of Blackie Barr that he could literally turn the air blue with his swearing; that he could stand in the Rocky Mountain House in St. Louis and startle a team out of their ox bows in Santa Fe, so thunderously loud were his bull-throated oaths.

But that had been before Raton Pass.

Steve Moore drove the Murphy ahead of Barr, soft-spoken, leering, deadly. And farther along, almost out of sight in the dust, was Rob Davis. He looked so much like the cattle he drove that it would have been funny to Blackie if he hadn't known how dangerous that big sullen bully could be with his terrible strength and his slow, single-track mind.

And in the lead, of course, was Raines. He rode his wagon most of the time, sitting up on the high box seat like some profane, chortling Buddha, handling his blacksnake with no less skill and ease than those who walked.

They made camp at twilight beside an old buffalo wallow some hundred yards to the west of the trail. Killdeer and snipe flitted about the rim, and bullfrogs boomed from the green slime at the water's edge.

The bullwhackers were usually in good spirits

at the beginning of the trip. There was always someone to fiddle or sing the time-honored "Dried Apple Pies." But this crew acted like a bunch of suspicious coyotes, muttering darkly among themselves, sulking about the fire.

Blackie was walking over to get his supper when sight of one man hunkering there brought him up sharp. Lean and long and spare the man was, a shiny bald spot on the top of his bony skull, a rapacious beak of a nose. Artie Hawkins, one of the men who'd whacked a team for Blackie in the train that burned at Raton. It was a memory from hell, and somehow Barr couldn't face it. He was turning furtively back to his wagon when Raines's voice rasped out behind him.

"Blackie boy, don't go off and leave us!"

The fat man waddled over and grabbed Barr's elbow in thick fingers, turning him forcibly, moving him toward the fire. Hawkins rose, bending forward with a strange expectance, hand caressing the ivory butt of a low-slung Smith & Wesson .44.

"I guess you and Artie'd like to squat and talk over old times, eh, Blackie?" chuckled Raines. "Yuh must have a lotta yarns to swap. About Raton, for instance."

There it was again—the same way Davis had said it earlier in the day. Blackie jerked free of Raines, impotent anger turning his face pale. Were they going to ride him like this all the way to Keeche? Hadn't they made him eat enough dirt?

Steve Moore uncoiled his blacksnake and began playing with it, slithering it across the ground like a snake, popping it playfully. He took a playing card from his pocket.

Art Hawkins smiled malignantly. "Cat got your tongue, Blackie? Why don'tcha say somethin'? Tell me how many wagons you burnt since those at the Pass."

Blackie whirled from Raines to Hawkins like a cornered animal. He hadn't thought it was in him, but they'd fanned the spark until reaction flamed for an instant. His voice came out choked, almost inarticulate.

"Damn you all! You think you can goad and kick me because I'm . . ."

A stunning detonation cut him off. Steve Moore's lash was just dropping to the ground, followed by two fluttering pieces of the playing card that had been snapped apart.

"That's it, Steve boy," chuckled Raines. "Show Blackie how you've improved since he saw you last."

Then he moved across till his sagging paunch was pushed up against Barr and the smell of him was oppressive in Barr's nostrils—prairie dust, stale sweat, and old sour leather all mixed together. He hissed when he spoke, and after every few words he took a wheezing breath.

"Now listen, Blackie. I thought Rob showed yuh how things stood, this mornin'. But we seen yuh talkin' to Miss Trevers afterward, and it made me think yuh didn't quite understand. Yuh ain't boss no more, see! You're just a lumpy-jawed, black-legged bullwhacker that takes his orders and likes 'em. So stay clear of the gal, and don't go pokin' your nose in any business that ain't yourn, or I'll have Steve here snap yuh apart like he did that playin' card!" Raines stepped back, suddenly chuckling again. "But you know better'n I do which bull to whack, don't yuh, Blackie boy? We're all right easy to get along with if yuh act smart . . . yeah, right easy."

Barr took a last look around the circle of hostile faces, lit bizarrely by firelight. Then he turned and walked heavily away, shoulders sagging. Why buck them at all? Pop Trevers had been wrong when he'd said Blackie Barr had the guts to fight back up to the top. Blackie had quit fighting a long time ago.

As he neared the outspanned Murphys, he heard bitter sobbing coming from the trailer of his own wagon. Circling the offside, he climbed in over the lowered tailgate. Rita Trevers knelt on her Mackinaw roll, dark head bent to her hands, slim shoulders shaking with sobs. At the sound of bolsters squeaking under Barr's weight, she turned distressed eyes toward him.

"I guess I just can't take it anymore, Blackie,"

159

she said. "Everything's ganged up on me. I'm so worried about Pop. Hunt and Lawler have been crowding us out up in Kansas. Pop had to get this contract or go bankrupt. He had to bid so low that he's losing money on the first trip. There's a time limit on the run, too, and if we don't make it, I think it'd kill Pop."

Yes, it probably would kill the old whang-hide if he lost his beloved freight business, thought Blackie. He'd built his whole life around high-sided Murphy wagons like this, with their musty beds smelling of black-strap sorghum, milled flour, and rolls of new crinoline.

"Pop isn't well," Rita continued in a low, tense voice. "He put everything in Raines's hands and sent me down later to ride with the wagons. It was an awful blow to find such a rotten bunch of Murphys, such a cut-throat crew. My only hope was that you'd be able to do something, Blackie. I used to stand at the window of Pop's office and watch you cussing your teams into line, thinking you were the most wonderful bullwhacker in the world. I put so much faith in the Blackie Barr I used to know. Then, to see you knuckle down to Raines and Moore and Hawkins, to see them laughing at you and treating you like dirt . . ." She broke off, shaking again with sobs.

Blackie felt clumsy and awkward. Finally, unable to say anything, he turned and slid out over the tailgate, her sobs fading as he went

160

toward the lead Murphy. Women had never played too big a part in his life. But he suddenly realized how much Rita meant to him. It only deepened his sense of defeat to know he'd failed her.

From force of habit, Blackie hauled his war sack out of the wagon and reached inside for the bottle, uncorking it and raising it to his lips.

He stopped, the bottle to his lips, without taking a drink. A nameless something was beginning to work deep within Blackie—something perhaps, that had been stirred by the pain in Rita's voice. It brought a thin, mirthless grin to his face, and the bottle made a sharp tinkle as it broke against the six-inch iron tire.

III

Shortgrass stretched gray-green as far as the eyes could see, and a flock of turkey buzzards wheeled above something in the distance. The wagons made a steady rumble, their creaking axles forming a thin overtone, punctuated now and then by a sharp whip crack. Those axles had already given Barr a hint of what was ahead. Before noon of the first day, it had become too apparent that practically every wagon in the train had not been greased.

They'd been forced to stop and waste precious

hours, breaking out two hogsheads of the tallow, rosin, and tar mixture used to grease the axles. No matter what else Raines was, he was a good freighter. He knew as well as the next bullwhacker that a hotbox was sure to result from dry axles, a jamming and sticking of wheels that would take half a day to repair. What was that sly fat rat up to, palming these creaking relics off on the Treverses?

Blackie's thoughts were cut off abruptly by the groan of halting wagons. Up the line, a Murphy was tipping far to one side, rear off-wheel crushed beneath it. Coiling his whip as he moved forward, Barr could see that a whacker was pinned under the wagon bed. The half-breed boy who herded the cavvy was tugging frantically at the man, brown torso bare and gleaming with sweat.

"You can't get him out that way!" called Blackie. "Get something to lever the wagon up with!"

Though his face was pale, the whacker's voice was amazingly calm. "I saw the rear wheel dishin' and tried to shove a jack beneath it. This is what I get. I'm not crushed yet, the axle's savin' me. But my legs is wedged in right snug. You better get that lever quick. The front wheel's goin' too."

Blackie could hear the slow groan of the tire slipping from that front wheel, the intermittent

162

snap of orange-wood spokes. If the man wasn't crushed now, he would be in a moment. Wondering why no one else was lending a hand, Blackie shot a glance under the wagon. There was no spare gear in the slings to use as a lever!

Impatiently he swung up the tailgate, ripping canvas from the rear hoop, jerking the high oak side boards from their sockets.

"Help me with this, wrangler!" he yelled, leaping down and jamming the panel beneath the wagon so that its two-by-four braces formed leverage. The boy added his brown shoulder to the oak, and together they heaved. The bed rose one inch, two. And with a series of grunts, the whacker pulled himself out from under.

With a sudden rending of crushed spokes and collapsing tire, the front wheel dished. Blackie and the boy leaped from under their lever as the big Murphy crashed down, smashing springs and bolsters, overhang digging into the earth beneath the weight of the three-ton payload.

The bullwhacker, a long, lanky man in red wool shirt and ragged brown homespuns, managed to stand, sweat dampening the hank of sandy hair that hung over his canny eyes, wind-wrinkles at the corners.

He knew how close to death he'd been, for he stood there a long moment, not speaking, face dead white. When he finally drew a plug of chewing tobacco from his shirt pocket and pared off a chew with a jackknife, however, his hands were very steady. He put away the plug and knife, pouted out his cheek with the chew, and stuck out one of those hands.

"Thanks, Blackie Barr. That was my life you saved. My handle's Squint Elridge. The 'breed boy here sort of tags with me. Found him when I was cuttin' wood in Kaintuck, and he's trailed along ever since. His handle's Choctaw."

Blackie took the long bony fingers in his, feeling a sudden warmth. It had been a long time since he'd gripped a man's hand that way, and there was a genuine gratitude in Elridge's eyes.

"Looked like Raines's boys were gonna let you squash," observed Barr, after shaking hands with the grinning 'breed.

The Kentuckian squinted, spat. "I raised a ruckus back at Caldwell when I saw what a lousy rig I was whackin'. Raines has had it in for me ever since. But I'm not his man, anyhow. Pop Trevers hired me in Dodge."

Rita had come up from her perch on the high box seat of Blackie's wagon, and she eyed the wrecked Murphy with a troubled frown. "This shouldn't happen so soon out of Caldwell."

"No," said Barr, "it shouldn't. Buffalo Creek's just ahead. We could take the wheels off every wagon in this train and soak 'em overnight so they'd swell tight into their rims. Unless we do that, they'll be dishing and collapsing all the way down to Keeche."

There was a reckless edge to Elridge's voice. "It'd be rubbin' Raines the wrong way. But damned if I don't vote we do it."

"Do what, Mister Elridge?" asked Raines.

They turned to see him standing there behind them. Despite his usual broad grin, there was an ugly glitter to his sly little eyes. Perhaps that was what so suddenly dampened Elridge's ardor. Now the Kentuckian spoke reluctantly.

"Well, Mister Raines, we was sayin' about the wheels . . ."

The same impulse that had made Barr break the bottle last night, made him break in impatiently now, a new note in his voice.

"We're swelling the wheels in Buffalo Creek, Raines."

Raines's grin faded. Patently, he hadn't expected this from Blackie.

Rita spoke up too, shooting Blackie a quick, expectant glance. "Blackie's right. You'll stop the wagons when we reach the creek, Raines."

"Now, Miss Rita," drawled Raines, "I inspected every one of them wheels before we left Caldwell, and if there was anything wrong, I'd be the first to know."

Something forcing him on, Blackie said: "Rita's as much your boss as Pop Trevers, Raines . . . and she gave you an order!"

The wagon boss turned back to Barr, cuffing the black hat back on his head in a baffled way. His sly eyes flickered over the four of them, noting that even the 'breed boy had something defiant in his stance. And perhaps because he wasn't prepared to meet this concentrated front that had taken him so unawares, Raines suddenly broke out in that affable, masking chuckle.

"Why yeah . . . yeah, you're right, Blackie. Miss Trevers's my boss, and whatever she says, goes."

After waiting an uneasy moment, as if expecting an answer, he turned and waddled back toward the lead wagon.

The train rumbled into Pond Creek Ranch on the Salt Fork of the Arkansas the next evening. It was a way station for the Reno stage, a log house backed by dark strands of timber. After a supper of sorghum and bacon and bitter black coffee, Blackie circled the corralled Murphys to Elridge's wagon. They had jacked it up back on the trail and put spare linch-pin wheels on. Squint Elridge was squatting beside the front one, inspecting the pins.

Barr made no preamble. "When I was hunting for a lever to get that bed off your legs, Elridge, I looked beneath the wagon for the spare gear. There weren't any. Since then I've been looking under the other wagons. There isn't a spare piece of running gear in this whole train!"

Elridge nodded. "That leaves us in a bad fix, don't it? Iffen we was to split a tongue, say, out in that open prairie country past the Arkansas, we'd have a helluva time gettin' another, wouldn't we?"

"You said you were a woodcutter, Elridge," stated Barr.

"Yup," the Kentuckian replied. "I do wood-cuttin' mostly, but I done my share of bull-whackin'."

"You could fell some of that timber behind Pond Creek ranch house," said Blackie, bending forward a little, "and I could help you rough out some spare gear."

Elridge squinted and spat. "Now, ain't you bucked Raines enough already, Blackie? He was plumb peeved when we swelled those wheels."

Barr grabbed the man's arm, pulling him erect. "Listen, Elridge, that fat wagon boss is up to something . . . I don't know what, exactly . . . but he's playin' havoc with this train. You shook my hand when I pulled you from under that Murphy, and you're the first man to do that in a long time. That's why I'm asking you to help me."

Elridge moved his chew to his cheek, eyes kindling. "I guess I wouldn't be standin' here iffen it warn't for you, would I? I'll do whatever you want, Blackie."

Turning to his wagon, Elridge drew out a whipsaw and a great double-bitted axe, sliding his hand along its hickory haft in what was almost a caress.

They picked up the 'breed by his cavvy yard, then cut around the ranch house, its yellow lighted windows casting square eyes into the night. Cottonwoods and aspens talked in a slight breeze, and finally they reached a clearing. Almost casually, Elridge lifted the big axe over his shoulder.

With no apparent effort, he threw it at a big hickory some thirty paces away. The blade dug deep and true into the trunk, handle quivering a moment in the pale moonlight.

Blackie grinned thinly. He was becoming increasingly glad that Elridge was on his side.

The Kentuckian set to work, his long awkward body taking on a surprising lithe grace as he settled into a slow steady rhythm. He felled and trimmed the hickory, then split it, and Blackie went to work with the whipsaw, roughing out a pair of wagon tongues and an axle tree. The herd boy hauled the crude pieces back to the train, lashing them atop the freight in Barr's wagon. And Elridge began on another tree.

The pot-bellied wagon boss had a surprise in store for him in the next few days.

IV

That surprise came sooner than even Blackie suspected. They were a mile below Pond Creek Ranch, fording the Salt Fork of the Arkansas— the broad brawling river that ran through most of what was known as the Indian Nations. The first half of the train was already across. Big Rob Davis was in midstream, lashing his animals brutally through the turbulent, waist-high water. Suddenly, laying a last vicious series of whiplashes across his oxen, he began to fight away from them.

Barr saw why. All six bulls had pulled loose, leaving the wagon and trailer to founder, high boxes angling over gradually into the muddy current. Squint Elridge had stopped his Murphy on the other side and was already plunging back into the water to help, but he was the only one. The other drivers on both sides of the ford stood indifferently by their outfits.

Blackie moved quickly, pounding past Steve Moore who remained deliberately idle, flicking his bullwhip and smiling nastily. Anger clawed at Blackie. Jumping between the wheelers of the team nearest the river, he roared at Elridge: "I'll unhitch this one and we'll haul them wagons out, tailgate first. And you," he snarled, turning to the others, "you help Elridge on the wheels or I'll bust your heads open!"

Four or five of them were surprised into obeying him, and they fought into the water toward the stalled Murphy. The yoked bulls lurched forward as Barr uncoupled the great center chain. He saw that Davis had completely deserted his team and was standing on dry sand, face stupidly blank.

Blackie broke into a blue streak of maddened epithets the old, thunderous, bull-throated cussing. He forgot everything but the bawling, sweating crazy struggle to save the outfit. Elridge had the men breaking their hearts against the wheels. Blackie whipped his team around in a circle and fought the chain over the trailer's rear axle, jamming the coupling bar through thick links. Twice he went under, bashed against the plunging oxen, choking, gasping. Finally he caught the wheelers ox bow and hung on, laying a veritable barrage of whiplashes over the leaders' heads.

The great beasts strained against their yokes, tails sticking out straight as whipstocks, mud spurting from under their hoofs. Spindles began to chuckle against thimbles in the big wheels; hounds creaked, bolsters groaned, and slowly, slowly, the wagon sucked out of the oozy bottom.

Elridge, sweating, swearing, and bellowing like a lanky demon in the pit, drove his men against those wheels with fists and boots until one of them threw himself down in the shallows, sobbing with utter exhaustion.

Blackie was on the bank, swaying against the muddy hide of his off-wheeler. He was dimly surprised to see the little 'breed driving Davis's loose team back onto the north bank with his goad, piping at them in Choctaw.

Raines had waded across by then, chuckling blandly. "Well, looks like a little trouble, eh? What happened, Rob?"

Rob Davis growled sulkily. "Damned tongue split clean through. Couplin' came out and those oxen like to rip theirselves apart gettin' clear."

Rita was there too, her face flushed excitedly. "That was magnificent, Blackie," she said. "It was like the Blackie Barr of old!"

"Yeah," grinned Raines. "You saved a good bit of money for Pop Trevers, Blackie. Get that sugar and flour and stuff in the river and it'd be a total loss. But we can't stand around here chewin' the fat, can we? Get your spare tongue on, Rob, and we'll be movin' ag'in."

Answering the mockery in Raines's voice with a knowing ugly-mouthed grin, Davis stomped to the wagon, bending under it as if he expected the spare gear to be there. Just then, Elridge walked through the group, dragging one of the tongues he and Barr had roughed out the night before. In that single instant, Raine was taken off guard.

Stunned surprise was in the sudden sag of his mouth, baffled anger widened his little eyes.

Big Rob looked up, staring at the tongue. He spoke thickly. "Where'd you get . . ."

"Yeah," the wagon boss cut him off quickly, regaining his composure with a perceptible effort. "Yeah, nice work, Elridge. Yuh always seem to be there when you're needed, don' yuh? Blackie and you make quite a team. Yeah, quite a team!"

With a hard look at Davis, Raine turned and waddled through the gurgling brown water to the other side, an angry hump to his fat back. And no affable chuckle floated to them.

Rita seemed to have sensed the play that went on beneath their words. She beckoned to Blackie to come away from the others. He walked beside her, off the trail a little, back toward his wagon.

"Raines didn't expect us to have any spare tongues, did he?" she asked. "And Rob . . . he could have saved that team from pulling free. He deliberately whipped them out of their harness when the coupling came loose of the split tongue. What are they up to, Blackie?"

"I don't know," he said, "but I can guess. Hunt and Lawler were crowding you out up in Kansas. It was them your dad bid against for this contract, and if we don't make it on time, they get another chance at it. Didn't Raines used to work for Hunt and Lawler?"

"Blackie, you aren't . . ."

He squeezed her arm hard enough to cut her off. They were passing Steve Moore's wagons. He was playing with his whip that carried the six notches on its stock for the men he'd lashed to death. His voice was a sibilant snake hiss.

"Right clever fella, Elridge. Knew just where to find that spare tongue. Friend of yourn, Blackie?"

Barr didn't answer. But he thought to himself: *No hurry, Steve Moore, no hurry. The time will come soon enough when I'll wipe that nasty smile off your face with the noisy end of my blacksnake.* And then, because the thought surprised Blackie, he rubbed at his unshaven chin. There did seem more of a jut to it!

The 'breed herder came back, grinning proudly, skinny brown torso still wet and glistening. "Elridge man, him say I good bullwhacker. I save Rob Davis's whole team."

"Have you got a gun, Choctaw?" Barr asked him.

The grin faded. "No, only Bowie knife."

"You better sharpen it up, then," grated Barr, " 'cause Raines knows whose side you're on, now."

It was five long back-breaking days between the Salt Fork of the Arkansas and the Cimarron River. Three axle trees came apart and a coupling bar broke. The train would have been held up for days, or would have been forced to leave the damaged wagons behind, but for the spare pieces Barr and the Kentuckian had roughed out.

Raines, of course, hid whatever he felt beneath his chuckle. He knew Barr was fighting him now, but apparently he was unwilling to bring things into the open, yet. They rumbled their ten or twelve miles each day across that endless expanse of gray-green shortgrass, and a subtle tension grew with every roll of the wheels. Art Hawkins began practicing with his ivory-butted Smith & Wesson, picking off the prairie hens or yellowhammers that flushed from beside the trail.

That tension even penetrated Rob Davis's thick skull, and he lashed his animals till he drew blood, looking about him defiantly all the while.

Rita asked Blackie to pack a gun. He didn't have a short gun, but strapped in its worn boot to his war sack was a lever-action Spencer .56. He dragged the war sack on top of the flour near the tailgate, where the rifle would be handy.

They arrived at Red Fork Ranch on the fifth evening. It was another way station for the stage and a trading store on the Chisholm Trail which came up from the Red River on the Texas border. The buildings were peeled-pole, stockade-style, earth banked up around their bases, barn-sash windows cut through the upright logs. A bunch of lean, bowlegged Texans stood in front of the store itself, their cow ponies hitched to the rack, heads bowed, trail dust of some early, northward-moving stock herd covering their tough hides.

As Blackie drove his outfit into the hollow circle of wagons, outspanning his team, he caught sight of Raines and Steve Moore galloping toward the timber that banded the Cimarron south of Red Fork Ranch. Blackie couldn't let that fat wagon boss out of his sight. He dropped his yoke irons, legging it to where the herd boy was driving the cavvy into some shortgrass browse.

"Get me a saddle, son. I'll cut myself out a horse!" he called.

The best mount he could find was an old sore-back mare, quite in keeping with the caliber of the rest of Raines's outfitting. Choctaw came back lugging an old stock saddle and a mecate. Barr slung the hull aboard and hackamored the horse with the mecate, then swung into leather and urged the reluctant mount after Raines and Moore who were disappearing into the cotton-woods.

Blackie lost them in the timber, but he took a chance and cut through to the sandy riverbank. Sure enough, their trail led southwest along that cutbank, hoof prints almost too easy to follow. He followed their sign carefully, stopping to listen now and then. It was habitual with Blackie to carry his Missouri bullwhip, but he so rarely carried a gun that he hadn't thought of getting the Spencer in his hurry to follow Raines. The snort of a horse and the sound of voices made him feel the lack of a gun acutely.

Blackie dismounted, ground-hitching the mare. A big patch of plum thickets stretched ahead. He crawled through them on hands and knees and reached a clearing. Raines and Moore stood breathing their mounts. The fat man was talking too loudly, chuckling.

"Yeah, Steve boy, I just can't wait till you and that Blackie Barr cross lashes. I wanna see you flay his hide off like you did that fella in Saint Louis."

Barr raised up and his breath caught when he heard a slight crackle behind him. He whirled to see Rob Davis standing there, a big brass-mounted Ward-Burton rifle leveled across his broad hip. Blackie's reactions had improved since he'd stopped drinking, and he threw himself violently sideways as Davis squeezed the trigger. Lead from the .50-70 whined past him and clacked into a cottonwood.

But as Blackie tried to regain his balance, Davis reversed the heavy single-shot, and with an animal roar, lurched forward, clubbing it down on Blackie. The rifle smashed into the side of his head with a stunning pain that drove Blackie to his knees. His last conscious thought was that he'd walked right into the sweetest trap Raines had ever laid.

V

Quail were cooing out in the clearing when Blackie came to. He lay there for a moment, trying to force his eyes open against the throbbing in his head. Dim light beat against him for a long moment before he realized it was dawn. He had lain here all night.

Cursing himself bitterly for the biggest fool that ever whacked a bull team, Blackie struggled to his feet, groping for his whip almost automatically. There was blood matting his hair, caked on his face. Groggily, he staggered through the undergrowth, hunting for the spot where he'd left his horse. They hadn't even bothered to round up the old plug. She was browsing within ten yards of the river, mecate dragging. He hauled himself painfully aboard and clucked her forward.

The bullwhackers were on the trail early, and Blackie knew the train would be far south by now. He followed the Reno trail through the timber on the other bank of the river, then through rolling sandhills and into more stands of thick aspen and cottonwood. Blackie was going pretty fast when he broke into the open, and he almost rode down the last wagon, stalled in the trail.

Blackie reined the mare to the tailgate, rising in

the stirrups and reaching inside for his Spencer. The war sack lay there where he'd put it, but the worn scabbard strapped to it was empty.

Slowly, he eased himself back into the saddle, looking for a long moment at the blacksnake coiled in his sweaty palm. It was all he had now. There was nothing else to do but kick the lathered flanks beneath him and go to the showdown armed with nothing more than this twenty feet of braided, tapered leather, tipped with a brass-studded snapper.

The men were gathered in a shifting, nervous crowd up by the lead wagon. They didn't see or hear Blackie as he came toward them. They were too intent on something within the circle. Elridge's dry voice cracked out above the other sounds.

"Raines, you great big pile of buffalo back fat, you done somethin' with Blackie Barr, and 'less you spill it, I'll take my axe to your whole crew!"

From his height in the saddle, Blackie could see over the men's heads to where Raines, Steve Moore, and Hawkins stood in a little knot in front of the other whackers. They faced Elridge and Rita who were backed against the Murphy.

Rob Davis shouldered his hulk through the bullwhackers, Ward-Burton across his hip. It bellowed, and Elridge bent double, thrown backward by the heavy slug through his belly. Raines, Moore, and Hawkins surged forward, and

Rita picked the first one to slap leather. Hawkins went down with the Smith & Wesson he would have drawn slipping back into its holster. The girl tried to lever a shell in, but Raines was on her, slapping the gun down.

Blackie was right in among them, now, mare's flanks knocking men right and left. There were few in the crowd who hadn't known the old Blackie Barr. And this man who swung down from the hipshot mare to stand with his bull neck sinking into heavy shoulders, dark eyes burning with a terrible light, deadly bullwhip laid out on the ground in front of him, was the old Blackie Barr!

The fat man threw a look over his shoulder, still fighting Rita. When he saw Blackie, he whirled the girl around in front of him, rifle caught between his fat forearm and Rita's shoulder as he held her facing Blackie. His right-hand Colt bore on Barr from behind Rita's blue-jeaned hip.

"I thought Rob killed you back there in the woods," rasped Raines. "There was so much blood around we didn't even bother to put a slug through you. Better drop the whip, Blackie. You can't get me without hurtin' the gal."

Rita must have seen in Blackie's set face what he intended to do, but she didn't flinch. She drew herself up, a shining, proud gleam to her eye.

There were whackers in St. Louis who made a show of snapping cigarettes from men's mouths at fifteen paces without so much as touching a whisker. Blackie had never tattled his yoke irons that way, but this was for Pop Trevers, for Elridge. Barr knew his skill with the blacksnake.

He bent forward, setting himself for that first slug from Raines, knowing he'd have to take it if he made this play. Then his arm moved in a blurred, backward-forward motion, leather snarling one way past his ear, then back the other way. Raines's Colt roared, then flew high in the air as the snapper on Barr's blacksnake howled past Rita's hip, an inch away from her blue jeans, cracking across the fat man's gun hand with a thunderous detonation.

Even as Blackie grunted with the pain of Raines's bullet through his left arm, he hauled his whip back into position. The wagon boss let Rita go and grabbed for his other Colt. The girl threw herself aside. Hugging his wounded arm in tight, Barr lashed out and cracked Raines's other hand as it gripped the gun, not yet unleathered.

The fat man choked out an agonized curse and flopped backward into a sitting position.

It had all happened in such a short time that no one else but Rob Davis had moved against Barr. Davis evidently hadn't taken time to reload his single-shot after gut-shooting Elridge, because as Barr turned with the pounding thud of charging boots in his ears, he saw the big ox of a man coming at him with the rifle clubbed.

Then a big gleaming double-bitted axe arced through the air, striking Davis just as true as it had struck that hickory back at Pond Creek—nothing else could have stopped the enraged man.

As it was, his momentum carried him against Barr hard enough to knock Blackie to his knees. Then Rob slid to the ground with a gurgle, rifle slipping from dead fingers, the axe handle quivering a little in his back.

From the corner of his eye, Blackie could see Elridge hanging onto a wagon wheel. The Kentuckian drew a shuddering breath.

"I figured I owed you that one, Blackie. It was about all I had in me."

He slid to a sitting position, shirt front covered with gore. Barr was erect again, turning to face Steve Moore.

The little man packed no gun. He was as proud of his skill with the blacksnake as Barr was. He stood there smiling evilly, braided leather out on the ground in front of him. Barr sent his lash hissing into the shortgrass, and that was the signal.

Barr saw his out-flung leather miss, by inches, as Moore dodged skillfully aside. And Moore's lash cracked across Blackie's face, knocking him backward, blinding him with pain.

Bellowing with rage, Blackie fought erect, automatically hauling his whip back into position, even as he pawed the blood from his eyes.

Then he could see again, and he was ready, legs spreading wider to support the forward bend of his square torso. Again those deadly bullwhips exploded into leaping, living things. Barr saw that other lash licking toward his face. His own leather snapped from behind his head. It met Moore's whip in mid-air, winding around and around it like an angry snake.

Muscles writhing down his hairy forearm, Barr jerked backward and Moore lurched forward, pulled almost off his feet, whipstock yanked free of desperate fingers.

Blackie freed the loose whip before it hit the ground. He lashed out again, catching Moore in that same position—bent forward, arm out, an evil smile frozen to his sallow face.

Crackling leather turned that smile to a welter of spurting blood. With an awful scream, Moore rolled into the dust, pawing at his face.

Blackie straightened slowly, panting, seeing what had held the other men at bay. Rita stood with her yellow boots spread wide, infinite threat in the Spencer held in her small brown hands. And beside Elridge stood the 'breed, Raines's Colts pointing toward the crowd. Raines sat on the ground, bent over his broken hands, moaning. Barr flickered his lash toward the man.

"Now, you coyote, talk! What was the game?"

Raines had taken enough of that whip; his words tumbled out in a rush. "O.K., Blackie,

O.K. Hunt and Lawler sent me. If they could keep Pop Trevers's train from making the time limit, they'd get the contract he beat 'em on. They didn't want any crude stuff, just delays that'd look natural. Pop Trevers was pretty desperate for help and it was easy to get hired. Even picked my own crew. Then you and that Kentuckian came along."

"When your train burned at Raton Pass, and Southwestern Freighting couldn't get another one through on time, didn't Hunt and Lawler get that contract, Blackie?" asked Rita.

Something unholy kindled in Barr's eyes then, and he took a menacing step forward. "What did you have to do with that, Raines?"

Raines jerked away from the flicking snapper. "Dammit, Hunt and Lawler put me on that one, too. Hawkins got a job whackin' for you so's he could work from the inside. Me, Davis, and Moore followed you to Raton. Then Hawkins conked the guards and put 'em in the wagons, and Rob and me dumped the water kegs so you couldn't douse the fire."

Blackie Barr could see again those charred bodies in the wreckage, could feel the awful sense of guilt that had hung over him, turning him into a drunken coward and sending him down the road to damnation. His voice shook with the effort to control it.

"I guess Hunt and Lawler won't be crowding

any more outfits in Kansas. And the least they'll do to you is hang you, Raines."

Blackie didn't say any more. He turned to where Elridge sat propped against the wheel. The Kentuckian's voice was faint.

"I reckon this'll be my last chaw, Blackie. You're a bullwhacker, and I like you. I'm a woodcutter mostly, but I done my share of bullwhackin'." With those words, Elridge tipped slowly, collapsing on the ground. A little tobacco leaked from his mouth; it had a reddish tint.

Blackie's eyes were too blurred with emotion to see for a moment. Gradually he became aware of Raines's men, crowding uncertainly around, lost without their leader. Blackie turned to them, raising his head, his voice husky and low when he first began to speak, but rapidly rising to a bull-throated roar.

"That was a man talking, you black-hocked sons of the coyote breed! By all the white bulls in hell, if you still think you ain't gonna take this train down to Keeche, I'll flay every stinking hide from this crowd and cure and sell 'em in Saint Louis for skunk plews!"

The men cringed backward. To them, Blackie's bloody Missouri bullwhip was the law now and forevermore.

Rita looked away from the still form on the ground, her eyes glistening. "We'll need the best wagon boss west of the Missouri to get us through on time. How about the job, Blackie Barr?"

It was in the girl's eyes that to her he could be much more than just a wagon boss. Blackie straightened, grinning despite the pain of bullet and bullwhip in him. The old Blackie was in that grin, and again folks would tell of how Blackie Barr could stand in St. Louis' Rocky Mountain House and startle a team from their ox bows in Santa Fe, so thunderously loud were his bull-throated oaths.

OWLHOOT
MAVERICK

I

Standing with his elbows on the bar, Johnny Peters heard the bat-wing doors swing open behind him, heard the heavy pound of boots on the saloon's unpainted floor. The three men sitting at the round deal table in the rear stopped their talk and looked up to see who had entered. Then the sound of boots stopped too. And for a moment, the only noise was the creak of doors, swinging back and forth to a halt. To Johnny, that hush held a sudden ineffable menace.

"I been expectin' you, Johnny."

The boy turned slowly, a tight, wary look entering his sun-darkened face with its big Texas jaw.

Don Thorne stood just inside the door, behind him two hard-faced, shifty-eyed men in alkali-whitened shirts and Mexican leggin's. Johnny felt Thorne's eyes regarding his face, his worn ducking jacket. His gaze stopped finally at his guns.

They were singular weapons, big, bone-butted Walker Colts in cut-out holsters, slung on a single broad belt that was strapped low around the waist of his brush-popper's cowhide leggin's.

Those Walkers had belonged to Concho Peters.

Thorne moved over to the bar beside Johnny,

189

followed by the two men. Johnny realized his palms were sweating, and he wiped them on his jacket.

"There's talk along the owlhoot that you're trailin' the man who killed your dad, Johnny," said Thorne, still looking at the guns. "I guess the talk's right, seein' as your wearin' his irons."

He was a big, bullying man, this Thorne; his black eyes set under beetling brows, nose large and hooked, marking all the grasping ruthless strength that was in him. His thick-fingered hands were spread flat on the mahogany bar, little scars criss-crossed over their backs. All the men from the Texas brasada were scarred like that, on their hands or their faces, or even their bodies. It was a harsh, cruel land, the brush country down below the Nueces.

A man couldn't ride ten feet through the mogotes of black chaparral without being ripped by the stiletto-pointed Spanish dagger, or clawed by the black-thorned palo verde, or stabbed by the tasajillo. Yet, it was the only land Johnny Peters had ever known.

His father had taken him into it when he was but six years old, after his mother died. The boy had grown to manhood, riding beside Concho Peters, his wild, untamed, almost legendary father. But though he was with them, Concho complied with the boy's firm determination not to take part in their owlhoot exploits.

A reckless outlaw named Thorne rode with Concho. But from the very first, Thorne had evidenced nothing but an indifferent contempt for Johnny, and there grew between them a deep, smoldering enmity.

Johnny couldn't help see that Thorne was too strong and ambitious to remain Concho's understrapper. One by one, he began winning over the men who rode with Concho, and soon the gang was split.

Yet, beneath all his wildness, old Concho had some good in him. He and the cowman, Ed Mallet, had been friends before Concho took to the owlhoot, and Concho never forgot it. Of all the cattle that Concho drew his running iron across, he never touched a Mallet steer. That caused the final break between Thorne and Johnny's father.

Thorne had always wanted to run off more steers than any longrider ever had before. He saw his opportunity in Mallet's untouched herds. But Concho balked at it every time Thorne mentioned Mallet's cattle.

Finally, Thorne made a break. He stood wide-legged in the little *cantina* at Jeminez across the border.

"I'm throwin' my brand on Ed Mallet's outfit, Concho, whether you like it or not. Me and some of the boys who think like I do are branchin' out on our own. It wouldn't be healthy for you to cut my trail from here on. I'd take personal pleasure in matchin' my guns with yours."

Now, remembering that threat, the boy felt a growing hatred for the big man standing beside him at the bar. He kept his voice even and soft when he spoke, but he couldn't help the twist in his mouth.

"What they say along the owlhoot is right, Thorne. Concho wasn't dead when I reached him. And when I asked him who shot him, he said that I should get to Ed Mallet. That's what I'm doin' . . . with Concho's own guns."

"Mallet's a pretty big man to go gunning after, kid," said Thorne. "You ain't even seen him before. You don't know what he looks like."

"If Mallet's such a big man, why'd he up and leave after he bushwhacked Concho?" asked the boy thinly. "I hit Mallet's spread. There was some greenhorns there from the East. They said he'd sold out to 'em and had hit the Chisholm Trail with a herd a couple of days before. . . . What does it matter to you anyway, Thorne? Don't you want me to cross with Mallet?"

"No," said Thorne, moving his heavy-boned face close to Johnny's. "No. I think you better turn right around and head back where you came from."

There was a malignant glitter in Thorne's black eyes. And Johnny sensed suddenly why the man had brought the two hardcases with him. The boy didn't know them, but he knew their type well enough—border rats who would do this kind of a job for a *peso*. Johnny didn't know why Thorne should want him killed; he didn't have to know. It stood as a simple fact—in Thorne's eyes, in the set faces of the other two.

The boy took his elbows from the bar and settled his weight solidly on both feet. "And if I don't go back where I came from, Thorne?" he asked evenly.

"You can figure that out for yourself." A slow, ugly grin spread Thorne's mouth, and his voice held the same deep threat it had that day back at Jeminez.

"I thought you'd refuse. That's why I brought these *hombres* along."

He turned and walked heavily back out the door, leaving the two men, one on either side of Johnny.

The man on his right was fingering his whiskey glass, not yet having drunk. His shifty eyes were on the boy's curling hands, on those twin .44's. Maybe he had heard of Concho Peters, and of his guns. He seemed to hesitate.

"You better get on your horse and do what Thorne said, kid," mumbled the man.

Johnny knew that words didn't matter now. The man was only keying himself up with the talk. Johnny set himself for the leap backward that would bring him in line with both of them.

"I'm not hitting any back trail," he said. "After all, Thorne's already paid you. I wouldn't want to disappoint him."

The gunny whirled, throwing whiskey, glass and all, straight into Johnny's face. Blinded, Johnny jumped backward, clawing at his guns. But even as they came out, he knew it was no good. He couldn't see, and he wasn't far enough back to cover both men.

So he made a wild guess at where the man on his right was, and thumbed both hammers back. His right hand Colt bucked and roared, then his left. He was dimly aware of other gun thunder than his own, and wondered why lead hadn't jarred through him from behind.

Then he could see, dimly at first. He must have beat the man on his right to the draw, because that gunman lay on his belly. The man behind Johnny was on the floor too, crumpled up and looking very dead.

Dazedly Johnny turned. Men were scrambling from behind upset tables. The barman poked a white face over the counter. And midway between bar and door, stood a tall, gray-haired man in dusty Levi's and checked flannel shirt, Texas hat shadowing a craggy, seamed face with twinkling blue eyes and a big, generous mouth. He must have just come in as the ruckus started, because the bat-wings hadn't yet swung to a stop behind him. His big, gnarled hand held a smoking short gun still aimed in the direction of the man who had stood behind Johnny.

"He would've dusted you off from back to front, sonny," said the man. "I couldn't stand by and see him do that."

For a moment, Johnny stood there, uncomprehending. There had been but one man in the world who would have done that for him—and Concho Peters was dead. For years, the youngster had known only the terrible, friendless savagery of the owlhoot, where a man stood alone. This was something new to Johnny Peters.

The tall man was ejecting his empty, reloading. "I guess we better hit the trail before the sheriff gets here. Comin'?"

Johnny backed from the room, not leathering his guns, but not covering anyone especially, because no one made a move. The other man backed out after him. Outside, on the walk of warped pin oak boards, he turned to Johnny.

"I've got a trail herd bedded down north of town. If you're goin' that-away, we might ride out together."

Johnny knocked the reins of his hip-shot lineback dun from the hitch rack in front of the saloon. "Yeah. I'm ridin' that way now. I'll trail with you outta town."

"Fine," said the other, sticking out a gnarled, rope-marked hand. "My name's Mallet. Ed Mallet."

II

Johnny knew his face had gone dead white beneath its tan. Ed Mallet—the man he'd come north to kill, and the man who had just saved his life. Belatedly, he stuck out his own hand.

"Call me Johnny. Yeah, Johnny."

By all the code of the owlhoot, he should have told Mallet his last name and why he was there. But somehow, he couldn't slap leather against a man who had just saved his life. He followed Mallet down the dusty street toward another rack in front of the courthouse, a two-story building with cupola and shake-covered gallery. There were half a dozen dusty waddies gathered by the tethered horses. Mallet introduced them casually.

"These are my boys, Johnny. Pedro, Al, Frank. . . ."

But Johnny wasn't listening because already he knew their names, had known them for many years. Pedro Chavez was a supple young Mexican, his hawk face somber beneath a giant rolled-brim sombrero. Al Blocker stood with his short bowlegs stuck in brush-scarred Hyer boots, looking as lethal as a snub-nosed derringer. Frank Hall was a tall rawhide rail of a man, his uptilted eyes and dish chin giving him a Satanic look.

There were other men, too, men who Johnny knew, for they were Thorne's men. And before Thorne had come, they had been Concho's men. Johnny had ridden a hundred wild rides through the brasada with them, had choused countless bunches of rustled beef with them.

Yet, now, they stared at him blankly, no sign of recognition in their faces.

A little crowd was gathering outside the saloon, and a portly man with a tarnished star on his serge vest hurried past the courthouse.

Mallet swung aboard a big gray, grinning wryly.

"I see Grantville is aroused. We better make tracks."

Johnny mounted his horse, a wary, half-wild look to his movements. He had a strange sense of suffocation, as if something were closing around him, inexorably. First Thorne, with his gunnies from the border, then Mallet. And now these men. He was acutely aware of their presence behind him as he cantered out of town beside Mallet.

They traveled a mile through the bunchgrass, green and sweet with early spring, and finally rode over the rise that bordered on the Red River, half sliding down the sandy slope.

To his left, Johnny could see the herd, bedded down in the bluestem of the bottomlands. The wagons were parked in a break close to the sandy cutbank. The night hawk was rolled in his sugan beneath the hoodlum wagon. A girl was talking to the ancient, pot-bellied Mexican cook.

Johnny saw that her eyes were big and dark as she looked to her father first, then to the boy, a candid interest in her smile. She wore buckskin britches with *pesos* for the conchos, and her pint-sized Justins had fancy red tops like a kid's first real boots. Her hair was as dark as her eyes.

"Jo," said Mallet to the girl, dismounting, "this is . . . Johnny. Johnny, my daughter, Jo Mallet."

The boy swung down, greeting her with a silent nod. He'd never had much to do with girls and her level gaze disturbed him.

"I'm glad Dad hired another hand," she said. "We don't have enough men to handle this herd."

"Well," laughed Mallet, "I ain't exactly hired him as yet. But how about it, Johnny? I need a jingler for my cavvy. Takin' along a bunch of saddle stock and it makes a pretty big herd. You'd free a hand to put on the cattle."

The boy looked from the girl to Mallet. It was the first job anybody had ever offered him, and it made him feel funny inside, somehow.

"Thanks, mister," he said hesitantly. "I guess I'd like the job."

Then a man came around from behind the chuck wagon. Johnny's face remained expressionless at the sight of Don Thorne. The big man stopped suddenly, and though his face was as blank as Johnny's, the youngster saw the boiling rage and a deadly warning glittering from behind Thorne's narrowed lids.

Mallet said: "This is my ramrod, Don Thorne. This is Johnny, Thorne. You can take him down to the cavvy. He's our new jingler."

Thorne wet his lips with his tongue. "Well, ain't that nice! A new jingler . . . ain't that nice?"

Johnny led his line-backed horse behind Thorne, down to the large herd remuda browsing apart from the cattle. Thorne stopped finally, and turned to face the boy. He shoved his flat-topped black hat far back, and put his hands on his hips. All the hate that was in him stood out on his face as if it had been put there with a stamping iron.

Johnny dropped the reins to the ground. He didn't think Thorne would try anything here, but he wanted his hands free. He spoke first.

"It isn't like you to hire two-bit gunslicks to do your work, Thorne."

"I've got a set-up here, damn you," said Thorne, voice shaking with anger. "I didn't want to spoil my chances by doing any gun work, personal. Nobody knew those border coyotes. It wouldn't have been hitched up with me. But now, by damn, if you don't climb aboard that crow-bait lineback horse of yours and leave, I'll cut you off pocket high, and I'll do it right here!"

"No, you won't," said Johnny flatly. "I come north to do something, and I'm not leaving till it's done."

If Thorne had been going to slap leather, he didn't, because Johnny's Colt suddenly loomed big and bright in his hard brown hand. For a moment, Thorne's hand twitched above his gun as if he would draw, anyway. But there was a cold deadliness in Johnny's eyes.

Thorne rasped: "All right. All right. You take this hand. But you've built yourself a tight you won't get out of."

He turned and stalked back toward the wagons. Watching him go, Johnny knew his life wasn't worth a plugged nickel if he stayed with this outfit.

Yet, he was staying. He was bucking Thorne on his own range. Grimly, he turned to unsaddle his lineback. It had taken hard riding up from the Nueces. He chose a likely-looking bay for a remount, its sleek muscle rippling beneath the satiny hide of its flanks, bottom in its big barrel. Heaving his rawhide-rigged saddle aboard and cinching it up, Johnny staked the horse near a pecan tree, then hunkered down in the shade, back to the trunk. And unconsciously, his hand slipped down to finger the bone-butted Colt at his hip. He remembered the last time he had seen those guns on his father. . . .

Concho Peters and Johnny had stayed in Jeminez for several weeks after Thorne left. But Concho seemed restless, drinking and gambling most of the time.

Finally he told Johnny: "A man don't stay alive long on the owlhoot when he gets soft, kid. I guess I'm loco, but Ed Mallet was my compadre, and I can't let Thorne throw any sticky loops his way. We're hittin' the trail north."

Concho never camped too near water. He said water was the first place another man struck for, on the trail. And a longrider found it healthier to avoid such spots.

So when Johnny and his father hit the Nueces River, they halted in a white brush draw to the south. Concho began gathering chaparro prieto for the fire, and the boy led the horses toward the river to water. He was almost there when the shot echoed flatly through the brasada.

Just one shot, no more, followed by silence.

Panic welling up inside him, Johnny ran awkwardly back to the draw. His father lay in the sand, blood reddening the back of his ducking jacket, rolled brim sombrero mashed beneath his face.

As Johnny ran toward him, gun flame lanced at him from the lip of the draw. With slugs kicking up sand about his feet, the boy whirled and whipped out his wooden-handled .44. He ran up the slope in a blind rage, emptying the gun. But when he reached the top, no one was there. The pound of horse's hoofs somewhere out in the black chaparral mocked him.

He slid down the bank and turned his father over. Concho was still alive.

"I told you they'd never do it from the front, kid. They had to dry-gulch me, damn 'em! Had to shoot me in the back."

He began to laugh, that eerie haunting laugh, like a lobo wolf howling its last call to the moon. But as it reached its peak, the laugh choked in his throat, and he began coughing blood.

"Concho," cried the boy. "Tell me who did it."

Concho had to force the words out with his dying breath. "Ed Mallet . . . Get to Ed Mallet."

Johnny knelt there a long time after his father had become a dead weight in his arms. He couldn't understand why Mallet should have done this. Yet, that was what Concho had said. Perhaps Thorne had already cut out some of Mallet's steers, and Mallet thought Thorne still rode with Concho.

Finally the boy rose, taking off his own .44. And before he buried his father, he unstrapped those Walker Colts, reverently buckling the broad single belt around his own lean flanks.

When he met the man who had killed Concho Peters, it would be with Concho Peters's guns. He would have wanted it that way. . . .

Breakfast was at five, and the herd of EM steers was on the trail before the sun had risen. Johnny choused his savvy along behind the cattle, the last rider in line. A big zorrillo steer began bunch-quitting early and kept it up all day. Along in the afternoon, he got past the swing rider, and galloped by Johnny, heading back for the Red River.

Johnny had ridden herd on rustled steers since he was old enough to fork a horse. It was automatic for him to wheel his bay and pound leather after the big black zorrillo with the white lobo stripe down its back. The animal sensed its pursuer and speeded up.

Johnny was urging his bay into a hell-for-leather gallop when something gave beneath him. He thought he'd blown a stirrup, and eased his weight over onto the other side.

He just kept right on going, saddle slipping with him. Wildly, he freed his heels from the stirrups, not wanting to be dragged, and threw his arms over his head. Then he was bouncing and rolling across the ground, pain shooting through him.

He crashed to a stop in some bee brush and lay there a long time, swimming up through a fog of agony. When he finally sat up, he saw that his ducking jacket was ripped from his back and rocks had dug long gashes from belt to shoulder blades.

The bay had stopped a few hundred yards farther on. Between the horse and Johnny lay the saddle. Rising stiffly, shaking his head, he stumbled over to it.

The broad, rawhide-laced girths had been neatly slit up under the leather skirt—cut so they would hold at a walk or an easy canter, but would snap at a hard gallop. Don Thorne would be sorry Johnny hadn't broken his neck. It had been so much safer than shooting a man in the open.

Johnny unbuckled the martingale and used it to repair the girths, stripping off some rawhide lacing and braiding the leather into the horse hair. Then he slung the hull aboard the bay, and grimly set out after the steer.

He rounded it up several miles farther on, getting in close to haze him back to the herd. Then, suddenly, he uncoiled his dally and fore-footed the animal. His bay stiff-legged to a halt and the steer somersaulted with a prodigious thump.

Johnny forgot the pain of his wounds, and his anger, as he snubbed the daily on his horn and swung down. The horse held the rope taut while he hog-tied the zorrillo with his piggin'-string. Then he bent to inspect the brands—for they were what had caught his eyes.

Perhaps an ordinary cowpuncher wouldn't have spotted it. Ed Mallet had missed it, apparently. But Johnny had ridden the owlhoot too long. He knew all the tricks. And as he ran his fingers across the EM brand, and spread the fresh hair away from the double bar trail brand, he knew suddenly what Don Thorne had meant when he'd said he had a set-up here.

They had already bedded down the herd when Johnny got back. He hazed the zorrillo into the herd, then headed for the chuck wagon. The Mexican cook would have some whiskey with which he could wash his wounds. They were all eating: Mallet, Jo, Thorne, most of the hands.

"Well," chuckled Mallet. "What happened to you?"

"My horse bobbled at a rattler and threw me," said Johnny.

Thorne's grin was ugly. "Bobbled at a rattler, eh?"

Johnny turned until he faced the ramrod fully.

"Yeah. Snakes never come out in the open to do their work."

Thorne's face grew dull red, and, for a moment, he seemed about to speak. Then he turned on his heel, jerking his head for Chavez and Blocker to follow him.

"Here," said Mallet, going over to the chuck wagon. "We'll see what we can do for them wounds."

Johnny stood silently while the gray-haired man swabbed at them with a cloth dipped in whiskey.

A battle was raging within the boy, a fight between trust and hate that had been growing ever since Mallet had saved his life. He knew it was the same thing that had torn his father, down there in Jeminez. Concho had violated all the rules he had ever lived by when he went north to warn Mallet—and he had died for doing so.

Now, Johnny wanted to tell Mallet what Thorne was doing, yet all his deep-seated allegiance to the warped, twisted tenets of the outlaw trail kept him from it. He told himself savagely that he would be a fool to help Mallet, if Mallet were his father's murderer.

So he said: "How long's Thorne been your top man?"

"Not long," said Mallet. "My other foreman got into a gunfight in San Antone, got shot up pretty bad, with a couple of my best hands. Thorne and

Blocker drifted along about then and hired on. There was another *hombre* I had lined up for my ramrod, but he disappeared. And Thorne was so good with the cattle, he just naturally got the job."

"I suppose he rodded your roundup and did the branding," said Johnny.

"Yeah," grunted Mallet. "I was busy drawing up the papers to sell my outfit down in San Antone. Thorne did a right good job, I think."

"Yeah, it was a good job, all right," said Johnny.

He couldn't help admire the way Thorne had engineered the thing, framing a gunfight on the former ramrod and two of Mallet's hands, corrupting the rest of Mallet's cowpunchers just as he'd corrupted the men who had ridden for Concho. He'd gotten rid of the waddies who were honest and loyal, working Blocker and Chavez and Hall in, until the whole outfit really belonged to Thorne instead of Mallet. He found a dull anger rising in him at what Thorne was doing to Jo and her father.

He jerked away from the man. "I'm all right now. I'll get another shirt and take the horses down to water."

He was standing beside his bay, watching the cavvy drink in the bubbling shallows of Cache Creek, when the snort of a horse behind made him whirl. He had his gun almost out before he saw it was the girl. She swung down from her buckskin, giving him a strange glance.

"What's the matter with you, Johnny? You act just like a suspicious coyote."

He grinned thinly. The Mexicans had another name for it—*cimarron*—the same thing they called the wild *ladinos* that roamed the brasada alone, running apart from their kind, wild and deadly.

The girl drew a deep breath. "It's nice down by the river, isn't it?"

He looked up, smelling for the first time the heavy fragrance of the white brush, seeing the golden blossoms of the huisache gleaming dully in the falling dusk. And suddenly he felt restless.

"How come your dad pulled up stakes in Texas?" he asked.

"That winter of 'Eighty-Six about wiped us out," she said. "He bought a spread in Wyoming with the money he got from selling our outfit to those Easterners. We're going to try and make a new start with these two-year-olds."

Watching her as she spoke, he realized suddenly how barren and bitter his life had been—as barren and harsh and vindictive as the brasada he had been brought up in. And he wished he could tell her what he really felt, wished he could express the emotions she aroused in him. But what was the use? He was an outlaw, a longrider. And he had come here to kill her father.

A dull, ominous thunder cut through his thoughts. He turned to look through the cottonwoods. The night was calm, bright with moonlight. But cattle were nervous, inexplicable critters. They'd stampede at anything—the rattle of the night hawk's spur chains, the flicker of a match to light a cigarette. And something had set them off tonight.

Johnny whirled, grabbing Jo, lifting her almost bodily into her saddle.

"Stampede!" he shouted. "Hit across the river."

He swung into leather, and side-by-side they broke into a gallop, splashing into the water. The cavvy was milling around in the shallows, and suddenly they too started running, spreading out in front of Johnny and the girl.

Looking over his shoulder, Johnny could see the vanguard of the cattle, pouring down the draw that led between the mottes of cottonwoods and into the river. Before he and the girl had reached the opposite bank, the steers formed a dark mass behind them, a mass that grew and grew, spilling out over the white sand and into the water, filling the night with a maddening, ear-splitting, earth-shaking thunder.

Johnny realized they were hemmed in.

The cavvy was bunched up in front of them. And the crazed herd of cattle was rapidly closing in from behind. As they broke through the trees, and into the rolling prairie, Johnny forced his bay over against Jo's buckskin, trying to urge it aside so they could get out from behind the horses. He managed to work the girl to the right flank of the cavvy before the steers reached them.

The leaders pounded in, sweeping Jo aside and into the open, but surrounding Johnny. He was a part of that wild stampede now, horns clicking and dipping in his face, cattle jamming up against his legs, shaking the bay. The ground trembled beneath him and that terrible, all-enveloping sound of two thousand galloping steers deafened him. He could smell the stink of every sweating hide, could feel the hot breath of the press right behind him.

The moon was high, and even through the rising dust, Johnny could see that other riders were outside the herd. Behind Jo was Ed Mallet, a tall swaying shape on his big gray. And back of Mallet was Don Thorne, shorter, bulkier, sitting his dun in a solid, arrogant ungiving way.

Moonlight glinted on the Winchester as Thorne drew it from his saddle scabbard. As Johnny saw Thorne raise the rifle and realized what it meant, all his allegiance to the owlhoot was swept away. He clawed his Walker out and twisted in the saddle, throwing down on Thorne. But the man was out of range, and even as Johnny got his first shot out, he knew he was helpless.

Thorne's gun blazed. Ed Mallet reeled in his saddle, then pitched over to one side and disappeared from Johnny's sight. Jo would be next, riding her buckskin up ahead of Thorne, and Johnny knew he couldn't help the girl unless he got free of the cattle.

He lowered his Colt, shooting at a steer on his right. The animal stumbled, fell. And Johnny forced his bay over into the space it momentarily left open. He shot again and again, dropping steer after steer, fighting his way gradually toward the outside, blasting his way free.

He saw Thorne take aim again, and he knew the same panicky fear he'd felt when he heard the shot that killed his father back there on the Nueces.

But Jo made a poor target, riding stretched out on the neck of her bobbing mount, looking back over her shoulder with a pale, terrified face as she raced away.

The big man sat up straighter in his saddle, trying to steady himself. His gun flamed again. The shot missed.

Suddenly Johnny emerged from the herd, guns empty. He came out in between Thorne and the girl, and already he was drawing blood with his big Petnecky spurs. The bay proved its bottom then, stretching out its long neck, surging into a killing pace that worked swiftly away from Thorne. The ramrod was throwing down for another shot as Johnny reached Jo.

Knowing there was only one thing that would

save her now, the boy freed his heels and jumped. He hit the buckskin on its lathered flank, grabbing at Jo. Together they rolled off the horse, Johnny twisting beneath the girl to take the full shock of the fall.

The last thing he knew was the heavy pound of Thorne's horse going by, the sharp crack of his gun above the sullen, thunderous sound of the herd—and then dark silence.

III

It was very quiet when he regained consciousness. The moon wasn't much higher in the sky. Jo bent over him, anxiety in her pale face.

"Are you all right?" she asked shakily. He nodded, sitting up with a groan. "You?"

"No broken bones," she said. "If you can walk, let's get back to . . ." She broke off with a stifled sob.

There was fear in her eyes as he rose and helped her up. Together, they limped back through the shortgrass toward Cache Creek, following the wide trail of the herd. They found Mallet, finally, crumpled up in a little swale where he had fallen, blood drying on his back. To Johnny, the sight brought back the sudden painful memory of another man, lying like that in a white brush draw, shot in the back.

Jo knelt and tenderly turned the lanky, gray-haired man over, cradling his head in her lap. Her face was white and set, her eyes glistening, but she made no sound. Mallet opened his eyes and a faint grin creased his face.

"I knew you'd be back. I knew you wouldn't let that dry-gulcher get my daughter, Johnny Peters."

Johnny hunkered down, and for a long time he didn't say a word, just looked at Mallet. Finally he muttered: "Then you knew all along?"

Mallet nodded. "I'd never seen you before, but I recognized you the minute I saw you there at Grantville. Concho and I was friends a long time ago, Johnny, good friends. But we both loved the same woman, and when he won her, our trails split. You bein' the son of my best friend, the son of the woman I loved . . . I felt almost like you was my own son. I knew you wouldn't gun me, Johnny. You got too much of your mother in you, and she was a good woman."

Johnny knew a bitter self-blame. If he had told Mallet about Thorne, this wouldn't have happened. He tried to lift the man.

"Come on. We gotta get you to a doc."

Mallet gasped. "No, Johnny. I'm dusted on both sides. It's no good. I don't see why Thorne bothered gettin' rid of me and Jo. If he wanted some steers, why didn't he just run off a bunch."

"He didn't want a bunch," said Johnny. "He wanted the whole herd. I found that out when I

213

was chousing a bunch-quitting zorrillo. When he put your brand on them cattle, he did it through a wet blanket."

Mallet raised up, choking out a curse. "Wet blanket? Why, that cussed polecat!"

The girl eased him back down and Johnny forced himself on. "Yeah. I guess you know the wet blanket trick. The burn doesn't go deep enough to last. About two months after branding, the marks disappear, the steers don't have no more brands on 'em than when they dropped from the cows.

"Thorne, I figure, planned to let the herd travel north under you until the scabs began to peel off and the hair grow back. That way he wouldn't be questioned. Then, when he hit Kansas and your brands began disappearing, he could get rid of you, slap his own brand on, and sell the herd at the nearest market.

"That's why he tried to stop me at Grantville. He figured I knew it all, and he didn't want you and me getting together, even for gun play. And when you hired me as jingler, he must've figured it was dangerous to string along any more. Good a way as any to get rid of us all . . . in that stampede."

"Well," said Mallet weakly, "he didn't get rid of all of us. You been shaped by the owlhoot, Johnny. It's made you like a wild animal. You're still young enough to change. There's other trails,

214

Johnny. Find yourself one. And take care of Jo. She's all alone now."

When Concho Peters had gone over the Big Divide, he'd gone out laughing that crazy, haunting laugh Johnny would never forget. Ed Mallet was a quieter man, but as he lay back in his daughter's arms, a faint smile creased his leathery face. They'd be riding another pasture together, the two men who had been friends a long time ago. . . .

Johnny stood, a bleak look in his sun-darkened face. He knew who had killed his father now. And when he got him, it wouldn't be just for Concho Peters. It would be for Ed Mallet, too.

They buried Jo's father where he had fallen, piling rocks over his grave to keep the coyotes away. The girl was mute and dry-eyed with her inexpressible grief. She followed where Johnny led like an automaton, moving dully, uncaring.

He had trailed many a *ladino* through the brasada, and it wasn't hard to follow his bay's tracks, leading away from the main course of stampede. He put Jo in the saddle and mounted behind the cantle, ranging north to find the buckskin. But evidently it had kept running with the herd, for they searched till dawn without any luck.

Johnny gave Jo a couple of hours sleep in the bottoms, then they mounted tandem and rode on again. Thorne probably thought they were dead, and the herd wouldn't be far ahead. They passed Fort Sill at noon, and rode on through the Keeche Hills, hitting the Washita River late that afternoon.

Johnny dismounted from behind the girl when they had reached the fringe of timber within sight of the river. He told her: "You stay here till it's finished."

She swung down. "Johnny, let me go with you. Dad's dead, now, and I don't know what I'd do if they killed you."

"Why should you care what happens to me, an outlaw, the son of an outlaw?"

"I care more than you realize," she said. "And you're not an outlaw any more. The owlhoot doesn't have any claim on you."

"I guess you're right," he said. "Your dad was responsible for that. I came north to kill him, yet he trusted me. Nobody ever trusted me before. Nobody ever thought enough of my life to save it, except maybe Concho. You trusted me too, Jo. And you've got to trust me now. You've got to stay here."

He turned and walked toward the river, raised heels sinking into the sand. The herd was strung out across the ford, point riders on the far bank, drag riders on the near. The animals were raising some dust and moving around a lot, and Johnny walked in close, unnoticed.

Al Blocker was languidly riding a sorrel not far off. Johnny was almost upon him before he turned around for a casual glance backward. His leathery, wizened face showed surprise, and Johnny didn't have to say anything. Those Colts in his fists were enough.

He jerked his head and Blocker dismounted. With one gun still on Blocker, Johnny untied the dally and lashed the man's hands behind him, then mounted the sorrel and swung over toward the other drag rider, leading Blocker.

Riding that sorrel, the rider must have taken Johnny for Blocker. Then he saw Blocker walking behind, but it was too late.

"Unstrap your hardware, Chavez," said Johnny.

The Mexican unbuckled his cartridge belt with swift, angry movements. "You can't jump the whole *quebradura* like thees, Juanito. Thorne's across the river."

"¡*Basta*!" snarled Johnny, reining over and jerking the man's dark hands behind him, tying them as he had Blocker's. Then he made Blocker mount behind Chavez, and they followed the drag of the herd across the river that way, Johnny riding behind the other two men. He counted on the dust and confusion to aid him in getting the rest of the longriders as he had gotten these two. And when he got the man who killed his father, he wouldn't use the rope on him.

But Thorne was the man who didn't take chances. He must have been keeping a sharp eye on the back trail.

Johnny splashed up out of the ford and into the dappled shadows under the cottonwoods. For a moment, he couldn't see very well.

"Stop right there, kid," said Thorne.

He was standing beside his horse in the shadows, a Winchester across his belly. Behind him was Frank Hall, his satanic face twisted with a certain satisfaction.

"Did you think we'd be dumb enough to let you round us up like you did Blocker and the Mex?" he asked Johnny. "You just don't know when you're up ag'in' your betters. Stubborn, like your dad."

"Concho was stubborn, wasn't he?" said Johnny. "When he told me to get to Ed Mallet, he didn't mean Mallet had killed him. He wanted me to warn Mallet what you was up to. That's why you dry-gulched him, wasn't it?"

"Reckon you're right," said Thorne. "Concho had some crazy idea that Mallet and him were friends. I knew he'd spoil my game, so I left Chavez to trail you north when you rode. I was already in solid as Mallet's ramrod when you hit the trail. Too bad I didn't nail you that night in the draw, too. You've been harder to get than Concho was."

"That's because I didn't give you a chance to

shoot me in the back," said the boy. "Want me to turn around now?"

The grin slipped from Thorne's face. "Get off that horse and leave your hands right where they are!"

The boy eased his foot from the stirrup. No matter what happened now, he was going to nail the man who had killed his father. If he dismounted in the ordinary way, swinging his right foot back over the mount's rump, it would put his back toward Thorne for an instant. So he was raising his foot over the pommel and twisting in the saddle to slide off, when the girl's voice sounded sharp and clear from the trees behind Thorne.

"Grab air, all of you!"

She didn't have a gun. She sat there beneath the trees behind Thorne, very small on the big bay, very harmless. But her voice turned Thorne for just that instant. And Johnny slid from his mount, his hands already filled with the smooth bone butts of the Colts.

They came out in that odd, one, two way— right-hand gun clearing leather before the left-hand one. Thorne whirled back, desperately, shifting the rifle.

But the shot he got out went wild, because Johnny's first slug went through his shoulder and jerked him sideways, and Johnny's second slug caught him in the chest, knocking him backward.

Chavez threw himself free of his horse. He had

219

worked out of his bonds, somehow, and as he hit the ground he dove for Thorne's Winchester. But Hall had his gun out too, and his lead smashed through Johnny's right arm.

Grunting with the pain of it, Johnny dropped his right-hand Walker. But the hammer of his other Colt was already rising and falling. Frank Hall took the bullet dead center.

Even as he nailed Hall, Johnny saw Chavez lever a shell into the Winchester and twist around on his stomach, bringing the rifle to bear. Johnny's thumb caught at the hammer, but he knew it was no good.

Then Jo was hurtling from the bay, landing with the full weight of her body on top of Chavez. He gasped. The rifle exploded in the air. And Johnny had his gun cocked by then.

"All right, Chavez," he said. "Get up. I've thrown enough lead for one day."

The Mexican got to his feet with a sullen, defeated look darkening his face. Other riders were pounding leather in from the herd, men who had ridden with Thorne, two or three of Mallet's hands Thorne had bought. When they saw the lean blond boy standing there with his smoking gun, they reared their mounts to a stop. But they had come in too fast, and his gun commanded them, now.

"Get off your horses," said Johnny. "And drop your hardware."

They dismounted reluctantly.

"Some of you *hombres* used to be Concho Peters's gang," said the boy. "Well, you're gonna be Peters's gang again . . . Johnny Peters's gang. And you're gonna stop those cattle and rebrand every one of them . . . only this time it won't be through a wet blanket. Now turn around and march."

He chose one of their horses, hooking an elbow around the horn and bellying into the saddle. The girl gathered up the guns, and they rode after the men, side-by-side, Johnny resting his Colt on the pommel.

"I thought I told you to stay across the river," he said.

"Did you think I would?" she said. "You can handle your guns and your cattle, Johnny Peters, but you don't know a thing about women."

"I've had practice with guns and cattle," he said. "Maybe you'll help me on that woman angle. Your dad told me to take care of you, Jo. I guess I'd like to. I guess I'd like to take care of you a lot farther than Wyoming."

She reached over and kissed him. "That's to make sure you will," she said softly.

BULLETS
BAR THIS TRAIL

I

When Tracy Bannerman saw the shadowy flutter in the dense stand of pines covering the slope above the Montana road, he could not help pulling the horses in. He felt Carol Hastings stir impatiently on the seat of the buckboard beside him.

"Why are you so jumpy, Tracy?" she asked. "Are you and Hal on a job?"

"What makes you think that?" he said.

"I saw Larry Coates in town yesterday," she said. "He wouldn't be down here for anything except borrowing money to pick up that option on the Golden Ace. And he wouldn't pick it up unless the mine had started paying off. The balance of the option is due tomorrow, isn't it? That's an awfully short time to reach Butte from here. A man Coates's age could never make a ride like that. So he put the money in the hands of the Bannerman-Wells Detective Agency."

Hal Wells was sitting on Carol's other side, and he turned in a sharp anger to say something, but Bannerman cut him off with a wry smile and a shrug of his shoulders. "Never mind, Hal. If she's figured out that much, why try and keep it secret? You're right, Carol. Trask and Company thought the Golden Ace was worthless when they gave that year's option to Coates. Now the ore has started assaying out fifty dollars a ton. The bank here wouldn't make Coates the loan, so he went to Doonhaven. Trask wouldn't take Doonhaven's check, so it had to be in cash. You can see why we were so reluctant to even give you a lift from town to your house."

She looked at the Gladstone bag on the footboards beneath Bannerman's knees. "Do you think Trask will try to stop you?"

"Tracy wouldn't get spooky over anything else," Wells told her. "Trask and Company have been running in the red themselves lately. If we don't pick up the option in time for Coates, the mine reverts to them. It would just about save their skins."

Bannerman had shaken the reins out again, lifting the horses to a trot. He was so broad he looked short on the seat, with his shoulders spreading remarkably beneath his sack coat. In the evening dusk, his square, aggressive face had a vague coppery tint, with dull shadows pooling the eye sockets beneath his brow.

Those same twilight shadows formed the shape of Carol's face, casting the rich flesh into a softened, satiny texture. The fact that she was Hal's, now, only seemed to intensify her beauty for Bannerman. *Like a kid,* he thought, *not really knowing how much he had wanted something until it belonged to someone else.*

She was a large woman, with black hair pulled back severely to a glossy bun at the nape of her neck, and a figure that shamed the painful cheapness of her gingham dress, beneath the wine cloak she wore. To Bannerman, that dress symbolized the poverty he would always associate with Carol.

She had been sixteen when he first met her, and in that very year, the hardships of the Hastings's barren Montana farm had killed her mother, leaving Carol to eke out an existence with a defeated, viciously frustrated father whose neurotic claims of ill health kept her with him even after she was old enough to leave. Carol's resentment of her circumstances had grown to a bitter hatred, focusing her mind upon the thought of escape until it had become almost an obsession. That side of Carol had always disturbed Bannerman, making him wonder when the breaking point would come, and just how far she would go to gain her ends when it did come.

Some movement from Hal Wells drew Bannerman's attention to the man. Wells was bent forward on the seat, staring up into the trees. The darting brightness of his eyes reflected even this fading light, and the skin of his face was drawn taut over the sharp angles of cheek and jaw by the tension of his raised head.

"You were right, Tracy," he said. "There is someone among those trees."

Bannerman drew the horses in so hard one of them squealed. He was shoving his coattails off the butt of his .45 when the man walked out of the pines. He came like a blind man, zig-zagging and stumbling down the slope into the ditch beside the road. He went to his knees there, and crawled up the shoulder onto the road itself. Then he fell full length in the muddy ruts, and lay still.

Bannerman's jaws ground together in a moment of hesitation. Then he shook the reins and set the wagon to rolling once more, halting it when they reached the man. Wells was swinging down before the wagon had stopped, the tall whipping length of him moving with the nervous vitality that never let him rest. Bannerman alighted more cautiously, taking a look into the timber on either side of the road before he went forward.

It was a kid of nineteen or twenty, lying on one side, black hair slickened from sweating, pale face smudged with dirt. Bannerman squatted down beside him.

"It's Eddie Saxon," he said. "I know his dad over near Helena."

The boy's eyes opened, lighting with hope when they saw Bannerman. "I was hunting in Belknap Cañon," he said weakly. "Using that old Sharps of Dad's. Stumbled. It went off at my leg."

Bannerman fished out his pocket knife and slit the blood-soaked leg of the boy's jeans up to the hip. Then he asked Wells to get the old blanket from under the seat of the buckboard. He cut this in strips for tourniquet and bandages. When he was finished, the bleeding had stopped, but the boy seemed to have lost consciousness. They got him into the bed of the wagon, then gathered at the front wheel.

"Shot himself," said Wells thinly. "That's a likely story."

"I guess we all know what a wild kid he's been," said Bannerman. "Whether he's telling the truth or whether he's in some kind of trouble, I wouldn't give him much chance without a doctor pretty quick. All that blood looks like an artery."

"It's fifteen miles back to Great Falls, Tracy," said Wells. "If we take him back, we'll never be able to reach Butte in time."

"Your place is only three miles, Carol," said Bannerman.

"Dad's in Helena with the wagon and won't be back till tomorrow," she told them. "There isn't anybody nearer than Great Falls with another rig. Couldn't you take him on through to Butte, Tracy? Doctor Miller is there."

"How could we do that?" said Wells swiftly. "What if a bunch of Trask boys jump us? What kind of clay pigeons would we look like with a man this bad off in our wagon? We can drop him at your place, Carol. He'll last till your dad gets back tomorrow."

"How can you be so sure?" she said heatedly. She turned to Bannerman with a soft plea in her voice. "Tracy . . ."

The heavy, square bones shone dully through the weather-stained flesh of Bannerman's cheeks as he dipped his head until his eyes were staring unseeingly at the road. Wells's boots shifted nervously in the mud.

"Forty thousand dollars, Tracy," he said, in a hurried, almost desperate way. "That's an awful big responsibility. Make it and they'll come flocking to you with deals. Muff it because of something like this, and nobody in the territory would trust you with another job."

Bannerman shook his head doggedly, knowing how right Wells was. It had been hard enough establishing the detective agency. It was not an unknown thing out here. The Rocky Mountain Detective Association had been established in Denver since 1863. But it was a hard pull for a man without much reputation or backing. Even Hal's gilded tongue had not moved mountains. Wells had come to Bannerman two years ago, convincing him what they could accomplish by pooling their talents. The man's personality and salesmanship had oiled the way to more jobs than Bannerman himself had been getting, but they had never gained the glittering goals Wells had held out at first. Perhaps that was why Wells's innate restlessness had grown so noticeable these last months. That restlessness had always been a doubtful factor in Bannerman's mind.

Carol's hand on Bannerman's arm broke into his thoughts. "Tracy," she said. "Could you ever face yourself again, if you didn't take the boy, and he died?"

Bannerman's chest swelled with a heavy breath. "I guess you're right, Carol. We'll take him."

"I'll go too," she said.

"Don't be foolish, Carol," snapped Wells.

She faced toward him, speaking with quiet, tight-lipped emphasis. "Hal, if there's going to be trouble, wouldn't it be better to have someone along to watch Saxon, and leave both of you free to handle it?"

Wells swung sharply to Bannerman, his voice savage. "Tracy, you can't. I won't let Carol come like this. . . ."

"What makes you so dead set against it, Hal?" asked Bannerman suspiciously.

Something like guilt fluttered through Wells's eyes. Then he lowered his sharp chin sullenly. "Forty thousand dollars is a lot of money, Tracy."

"It is, Hal, it is." Bannerman studied Wells's face narrowly. "It can make a man's eyes bigger than his stomach, sometimes."

"Now what are you talking about?" asked Wells.

Bannerman turned to climb into the wagon, saying nothing.

II

The road ran southward, past the Hastings farm near the Little Fork cut-off, paralleling the Missouri all the way. The river filled the coming night with the roaring sound of its intumescent spring tides, and on the other side of the road, tamarack backed densely into the foothills, dripping incessantly from the earlier rain. Bannerman drove the buckboard, working at the team in grim silence whenever the viscid mud fought the front wheels and set the tongue to whipping.

They had made a makeshift bed of hay and blankets for the wounded boy, and Carol sat back there with him. Soon, Bannerman became aware of Wells's eyes on him, and turned an oblique glance to the man.

"What's on your mind, Hal?"

"Nothing much," answered Wells.

"Mad about this?"

"Aren't you?"

"I guess I am, Hal. Nothing else on your mind?"

"Lot of things. This trip isn't going to be any vacation."

"I didn't mean that." Bannerman watched the trotting horses darkly before he spoke again. "You know, Hal, we've been working together in this agency over two years now. Yet sometimes I feel as if I don't know you at all."

"There's parts of every man nobody will ever see," said Wells, emitting a sharp, humorless chuckle. "Maybe they'd be sorry if they did."

"I guess you're right," Bannerman told him. "Don't ever make me sorry, Hal."

Wells's head turned toward Bannerman so abruptly it caused his body to shift against the seat, creaking the boards. But Bannerman did not elaborate, and finally Wells settled back. Light from the rising moon glistened on the poplar leaves and turned the water in the muddy ruts to copper. The laboring wheels groaned against their axles. A horse snorted fretfully and tossed its head. These were the only sounds as the miles passed behind, until almost midnight, when they reached the way station at Bird Tail Divide.

The lighted windows threw elongated rectangles across the road in front of the building, bright as yellow paint, and Bannerman was reluctant to reveal the wagon by pulling into this illumination. He drew the team to a halt in the shadows of the corral, fifty feet from the front door.

"I guess all of us could do with something hot, Hal," he said. "Want to get it?"

Wells did not try to hide his reluctance as he stepped off. There was the muffled hiss of clothing against Carol's shifting body, behind

Bannerman. Then the spring seat was depressed beneath her settling weight.

"Mind if I sit up here and stretch a bit?" she said. "Gets a little cramped back there."

"I imagine," said Bannerman. "How is the boy?"

"Resting easy."

He did not realize how closely he was watching her until, in some self-conscious gesture, she reached up to smooth the cloak down over one shoulder.

"It's a pretty cloak," he said.

"Tracy, you don't have to be like that."

"I mean it," he said.

"It's just an old hand-me-down so thin it doesn't keep me warm any more. Now stop it."

"It's still a pretty cloak," he said quietly. "A gunny sack would look pretty on you."

Moonlight caught the flush rising into her face. "Will you never understand what those things can mean to a woman?"

"Maybe I understand better than you realize, Carol," he said.

She turned partly away, with the old contention rising between them to mar the moment. Bannerman studied the curve of her cheek, knowing a poignant wish that he could give her his values in the judgment of things. He often wondered, actually, what values Hal Wells had given her, wondered how much her choice had been due to Hal's glib tongue, and how much to the man himself.

"I've never blamed you for your desire to escape your present circumstances, Carol," he said softly. "I never even blamed you for turning me down because I couldn't give you what you wanted. You've had a bitter time. I only hope it hasn't twisted your conception of things enough to drive you into something you'll be sorry for."

"It isn't like you to talk this way," she said.

"I wasn't implying Hal," he said. "I've already accepted the fact that you will marry him, Carol, if that's the way you want it."

"Then what were you implying?"

He frowned at her in a puzzled way. "I don't know," he said. Then he found his eyes drifting to the Gladstone bag beneath his legs, and it struck him how similar Carol and Wells were in their driven need to rise above their present circumstances.

"How did you happen to pick this particular day to be in town?" he asked. "You always shopped on Wednesday before."

"Tracy," she said irritably, "you're acting very strangely."

He shrugged. "I'm sorry. If we make this job, it will be a nice fee. Hal has already hinted he's going to pull out afterward. Where will you go?"

"Denver, as soon as we're married. Hal says there's a lot going on there. A man with a little capital could do big things. When we're able, we'll send for Dad." Her eyes shone a little, and he knew the visions that were passing before them. Then a shadow blotted out the glow, and she turned to him with a darkening doubt in her face.

"Tracy," she began. "Hal . . ."

He waited for her to go on, and when she did not, asked her: "What about Hal?"

"He didn't want to take the boy."

"Neither did I, Carol."

"But you gave in. If it had been up to Hal, he wouldn't have taken Saxon at all."

Bannerman shrugged. "Don't blame Hal. I'm sure, if he'd stopped to think . . ."

"Are you, Tracy?"

The tone of her voice focused his eyes sharply on her face. Before he could define what was there, Wells came from the way station with the coffee. They drank it quickly, and he took the cups back. When he climbed into the wagon once more, Bannerman gave him the reins.

Beyond the way station was Bird Tail Divide, where the resinous scent of balsam poplars tainted the air like cheap perfume. Bannerman sat silently, jerked this way and that, by the jolting wagon, listening to the muttered cursing of Wells as the man fought the team across rough stretches, the death rattle of wind through the thistle on exposed turns. Bannerman's whole awareness resided in these sounds, sifting them out, identifying them, waiting, always, for the foreign element. He could not have told the actual moment it finally reached him. They were on the other side of the divide, dropping down fast, with the brake shoes squawking like raucous birds under Wells's incessant braking, when Bannerman straightened up in the seat.

"What is it?" asked Wells.

"Feels like the ground shaking."

Long association with Bannerman's sensitivity for danger caused Wells to brake hard, pulling in the team as they swung down out of the last grade into the stagnant shadows of the hollow. The wagon was not completely halted when it burst upon them—a burgeoning tide of sound and movement exploding from the night to sweep over them and bring Wells up in the seat.

"There must be a hundred of them!" he shouted, half-risen. "What'll we do, Tracy?"

Bannerman grabbed his arm, calling sharply to him. "Just sit tight. This is too many for Trask."

Already the horses were flooding in around the wagon, smashing up against it as their riders drew them to a violent halt. The buckboard swam in a sea of lathered rumps and marbled eyes. The glitter of gun metal fluttered through the crowd like sunlight reflected from a brassy sea. A rider came forcing his way in from the outer ranks, calling to Bannerman.

"Speak up. Who are you?"

"Tracy Bannerman," answered the detective. "On my way to Helena."

The rider had come in close enough for Bannerman to see, now. He was immense and bear-like in a shaggy sheepskin coat. Sweat made greasy channels of the deep, weathered lines forming his unshaven jowls.

"What's in the back?" he asked officiously.

"We've got a wounded man," said Bannerman.

"A wounded man!" It was almost a shout. "Keno, give me a light."

"What's the matter?" said Bannerman. "Who are you men?"

"I'm Con Fallon from Lodgepole. This is a posse with me, mister. Carney Rolph's bunch just held up the Helena stage and got away with a big chunk of Butte payroll money. Two people on the stage were murdered. One of them was a woman. . . ."

The flare of a match cut him off. In its indefinite sphere of light, the face of the man named Keno was turned to a weird shadow-pocketed mask, as he leaned out of his saddle to stare into the buckboard.

"That's him," said Keno. "I'd swear it. He's the one I shot!"

The buckboard shuddered with the wild swirling

motion that broke out anew among the riders, carrying their horses against the wagon from every side. There was something bestial to their hoarse voices as they shouted at each other, shaking their guns in the air.

Bannerman's whole body gathered itself.

Wells caught his arm, pulling him back to hiss in his ear: "Take it easy, Tracy. A payroll robbery means greenbacks. If you cause any trouble, they're liable to find this money on us."

The threat of that held Bannerman for a moment. Then he saw one of the men taking a rope from his saddle whangs and passing it through the riders. There was a hang noose on it.

"You can't be that sure of this!" shouted Bannerman, hauling up against Wells's frantic hand. "Where was that stage held up, Fallon?"

"Tracy," Wells's voice was hardly audible over the surf of sound. "If this bunch is set for a hanging, you can't stop them. You know how crazy they are to get hold of Carney Rolph's gang in Helena. For the things he's done, I'd hang him myself. For God's sake, don't get us mixed up in it."

The man named Keno was swinging down off his horse, along with another, and climbing into the stern of the wagon for the boy.

"Fallon!" shouted Bannerman, fighting from Wells now. "If that was the Helena stage they robbed, it couldn't have been earlier than four-thirty. We picked this man up ten miles south of Great Falls at six o'clock this evening. He couldn't have gotten that far in so short a time."

"What's your interest in this, mister?" Fallon asked hoarsely. "How do we know you ain't one of the Rolph bunch too? What have you got in that Gladstone?"

Carol's sharp cry wheeled Bannerman about to see that Keno had flung her backward from where she had been crouched above Eddie Saxon, trying to protect him. She staggered into Bannerman and went to her knees. Her face was like the fixed, waxen mask of a doll, turned upward toward Hal Wells. There was terror in her eyes, but behind that was a strange, searching little light. Wells did not even see her.

"Tracy, please," he said, clinging to Bannerman's arm with hands so sweaty the sleeve was wet. "This is a lynch mob. Can't you see it in their faces? They're crazy for it. If they find that money on us, they'll lynch us, too. For heaven's sake, now, he's a murderer, don't be a fool."

That light seemed to fade in Carol's eyes. They became as blank, as soulless as stones in her head, as she stared up at Wells.

"Come on, damn it," said Keno, tugging at Saxon.

The boy groaned, as they started sliding him out the rear. Carol's eyes were on Bannerman now. There was no expression left to them. She was just watching him. Bannerman tore Wells's hand free and jumped over Carol.

"Tracy!" screamed Wells.

Bannerman's jump carried him to Keno before any of the men in the crowd could line up a gun on him. Then they were afraid to shoot, for fear of hitting Keno and the other man in the wagon. Bannerman used that fact, throwing himself between them and pulling at his Bisley. Keno tried to straighten up from the wounded boy, but Bannerman caught his elbow with a free hand, swinging him around hard and jabbing the gun into his back.

Keno's efforts ceased abruptly. The sound seemed to die, too. At first, Bannerman thought it was what he had done here. Then he realized Keno was looking at something up front, and so were the men along the inner ranks of horsemen. Bannerman must have kicked it off the seat when he jumped for Keno. The Gladstone bag lay on its side in the bed of the wagon, and it had come open, to spill out a stack of fresh green bills.

"The money!" The husky restraint of Fallon's voice sounded strange, after all the shouting. "They had the money right there beside them all the time. . . ."

The sudden bedlam of sound drowned his voice. The wild shouting of men, the squeal of frenzied horses, the splintering of wood in the wagon as it shuddered and tilted under the battering of the animals in a renewal of the crowd's violent eddying. Bannerman stood holding the Bisley to Keno's back, his whole body raised up with the expectancy of that first shock of bullets from a dozen guns pointed at him. Slowly, however, the noise faded, until he could be heard.

"I'm glad you don't want to kill your friend here that way," he said. "Now, which one of you is the sheriff?"

"There ain't no sheriff," Fallon told him, rage swelling his throat.

"You're doing this without the law?" asked Bannerman.

"Sheriff's over in Lodgepole Cañon with another part of the posse," Keno said hoarsely.

"I want one of you to ride for him," Bannerman told Fallon.

"Won't be necessary," offered a caustic voice. "He's done come."

The horsemen parted before that voice. It revealed a long, dour man with a mustache like Spanish moss drooping from his upper lip. He was followed by a line of horsemen coming single file out of the timber, and he kneed his Choppo horse in through the steaming press to the wagon.

"Thought I'd better check up on you, Fallon," he said, squinting one jaundiced eye at the man, "before you got het up and hung the wrong party."

"But this is the whole Rolph gang, Holmes!" shouted Fallon pompously. "They've got the wounded man and the money. . . ."

"Ain't no wounded man," interposed Sheriff Holmes. "He's dead. Cashed in his chips right in the middle of the Lodgepole road. We found all the money on his horse. So now, Fallon, if you'll turn your self-appointed vigilante committee around and drag your spurs for home, I'll give this fellow in the wagon one good, clear shot at your back."

III

Beyond Bird Tail Divide was Prickly Pear Valley, a moon-swept expanse of grain fields and snake fences. Soon the moonlight drowned in the bat-blackness preceding dawn, and then, as this began to turn gray, the rain-dampened land started steaming with anticipation of the sun's warmth. Piegan Rock jumped out of the fog-shrouded gloom at the wagon, and Bannerman pulled up here. Though he could not see the Big Belt way station ahead, he knew it was about fifty yards beyond the rock.

"Why don't you go on in, Tracy?" grumbled Wells, stirring stiffly on the seat. "We all rate a little stretch and a good hot meal."

"I'll still play it safe," said Bannerman. "Too

many men in that vigilante committee saw this money, and Trask hasn't made their bid yet. You and Carol go inside if you want."

Wells climbed down off the buckboard and turned toward Carol. "I'll help you down."

"I'll stay here," she said.

"Carol, you look tired. Tracy can watch Saxon."

"I'll stay here."

"Carol, will you get out of that wagon?"

"Why are you so anxious for me to come in, Hal?"

Something entered Wells's face that Bannerman had never seen before. For a moment, he thought Wells was going to reach up and grab Carol. Then the man wheeled in a sharp, vicious way and walked toward the buildings. Within a few feet, the fog had swallowed him.

"Tracy," said Carol, from behind, "will you get out of the wagon now?"

Bannerman turned to see her father's derringer in her hand—pointed at him. At the blank disbelief in his face, a tight look pinched in her eyes.

"Did you think Hal was the one who would double-cross you, Tracy?"

"Carol . . ."

"Never mind. I know you did. It's been in your mind from the beginning. There's no time to talk, now. Get off the wagon and take that bag with you."

He did as she asked. She got down and jerked the gun toward the opposite side of the road. Gray serpents of fog lashed at his legs as he walked over there, climbing into the deep ditch at her bidding. She followed, tearing her skirts on the rocks. Then Bannerman heard the quick, nervous thudding of Wells's boots coming back.

"Tracy?" he called softly. Then his voice lifted in a surprised stridor. "Tracy, where are you?" He climbed up on the wheel, looking into the bed. "Tracy," he shouted, "where are . . ."

A shot made a muffled detonation in the smothering fog. Wells dropped off the wagon, ducking back of a wheel.

"Norton," he called. "Stop. It's me, Wells. They're gone."

There was a moment without sound, then the hurried, crushed sibilance of feet running on fallen underbrush. Finally a wraith-like figure appeared at the tail of the wagon. A sliver of wet light ran along the barrel of a rifle swinging in one hand. The voice was thin and sharp.

"What happened?"

"I don't know," said Wells. "They were here when I left, just like I told you at the station."

"The hell you say, Hal. So you had it all figured out, did you? Keep me up by the station while they get away with it."

"No, Norton," said Wells. "I swear . . ."

"You're always swearing, but I never heard you

245

cuss yet!" shouted Norton. "Trask will have my hide for this. I could have got Bannerman if it wasn't for you."

"Norton, I tell you, I didn't know they planned this. . . ."

Wells grabbed the end of the rifle barrel as Norton tried to swing it toward him.

Bannerman realized the pressure of Carol's gun was no longer against his back and half turned his head for a glance at her. She was looking at him with a strained, waiting expression on her face.

With a sick intuition of what was going to happen, Bannerman turned back to the struggling figures and started scrambling up out of the ditch, pulling his own Bisley.

Norton finally jumped backward, tearing the rifle from Wells's grasp.

"No, Norton!" cried Wells.

Bannerman had that one shot, and he aimed high so the bullet wouldn't go through the wagon and hit the wounded boy.

Wells made no move to go for a gun, or anything else, as Bannerman ran toward him. Norton's face was made unrecognizable by the blood covering his head. He was dead.

"Was there going to be any shooting the way you'd planned it, Hal?" asked Bannerman.

"No, Tracy, I swear. . . ."

"I believe you, Hal. It takes guts to plan on shooting." Bannerman drew in a slow, tired breath.

"Sounds like some of the station crew coming now. I don't want to waste time explaining. We're behind schedule as it is. You stay and explain, Hal. Tell them the truth. Tell them this man was hired to stop me from doing a job. They'll probably hold the inquest at Helena. Sheriff Holmes will know where to get me if they want me."

"But, Tracy, what about me?"

"They won't have anything to hold you for," said Bannerman. "Get out of Great Falls, Hal. That's all I ask."

Carol had brought the Gladstone bag, and after Bannerman climbed into the wagon, she set it on the seat. Wells started to speak. She took one glance at him, then turned and climbed up to the buckboard. The station crew shouted at them as the wagon passed, going down the road, but Bannerman did not answer.

"Maybe you should have left me back there with Hal," Carol said finally.

"You knew what he planned to do?"

"Yes," she said. "You can see why I didn't have time to do any explaining in the wagon. I didn't know how soon they would come. Hal never let me in on the details of their plans, but I did know he meant to have this money. When he was so insistent that I go with him to the way station, I figured this was the spot."

"Their plan was fairly obvious, I think,"

murmured Bannerman. "Hal met Norton up by the building, told him the lay of the land. Then Hal was to come back, wait till some noise from Norton out in the timber attracted my attention, and hit me over the head from behind."

"I imagine it was something like that, Tracy. I was sure Hal didn't mean to have you shot, or I wouldn't have been willing to go through with it. I guess that doesn't excuse me. The fact remains that I was willing. Can you understand that?"

"I told you I never blamed you for wanting to escape your present circumstances, Carol," he said. "The kind of time you've had could twist anybody's sense of values."

"I guess what happened tonight straightened out that sense of values, Tracy. When they were going to lynch Saxon, and Hal was pleading with you to stay out of it, I saw myself very clearly, in him."

"It isn't too late," he told her. "This fee will be good, Carol, but it won't make me rich. I can't offer you any more than I did before."

Her eyes were shining. "It will be more than enough, Tracy."

DEAD MAN'S
JOURNEY

I

Ray Bandelier fought his way by the fringe of the crowd in front of Sacramento's Lyceum theater and ducked down the alley. He got as far as the stage door, then sagged against the wall, drained by the exhaustion of his run.

Behind him he could hear the hubbub typical of Sacramento in the spring of 1859—the creak and rattle of buggies fighting their way through the swarms of miners and gamblers and emigrants in the streets, the cries of the men at the sidewalk thimble and strap games, the spiel of shills in front of the saloons. As Bandelier tried vainly to recognize sounds of pursuit in this, the stage door was flung open, and a kettle-bellied man in a black frock coat stepped out, laden with bundles and suitcases.

Bandelier tried to turn back toward the street, but his legs were rubber, and he fell against the wall. He would have gone down if the other had not dropped his load and lunged forward to catch him. Bandelier had a glimpse of a florid face under a bell-crowned hat and a sweeping mane of inky-black hair distinguished by the iron-gray at its temples. The eyes had a dramatic, burning quality, despite the red-rimmed, bloodshot look of a heavy drinker.

"When the wine's in, the wit's out, young man. Did they swindle you in that den of iniquity next door and then bounce you out?" His eyes narrowed, and he peered closer. "Or maybe it's something else . . . Mister Bandelier."

Bandelier could not help stiffening against the wall in surprise. He made a tall figure, even bent over as he was. There once might have been a keen refinement to his face, with its long jaw, its high intelligent brow. But now the three-day growth of black beard and the starved look hollowing his cheeks gave him a frayed, beaten look.

"You're mistaken," he said, trying to get loose. "I got in here by accident."

"Accident, hell," snorted the other. "I heard about the murder today. They say you killed Henry Jordan in his office. They've been turning the town upside down for you." He emitted a rueful snort. "It's funny. When I heard the man who killed Jordan was Ray Bandelier, I never connected it with the Bandelier who acted the best Hamlet outside of Booth, at Wallack's two years ago."

Bandelier straightened up, a strange, tense look crossing his face. "You saw me?"

"More than once," answered the man. "You've changed a lot. I guess I wouldn't have recognized you if I hadn't connected the names." He studied Bandelier's face carefully. "Did you really kill Jordan?"

A sullen defiance lit Bandelier's eyes. "You wouldn't believe me if I told you."

The man squeezed his arm. "Try me, son, try old Louis Calvert. We troupers have to stick together."

Bandelier brushed shaggy hair off his brow, a plea filtering into his face. "All right. I didn't kill Jordan. I've been prospecting out here a couple of years and found something good up on the Yuba. Jordan grub-staked me till he found I had pay dirt. I came down today to get enough money to finish developing the mine. Jordan had the money there, but said he wouldn't give it to me till I signed a contract. It didn't take a lawyer to see that contract would have pinched me down to nothing." Bandelier shook his head. "I guess I got pretty mad. We fought. I knocked him over the desk. But he was only unconscious when I left. I swear that, Calvert. He wasn't dead."

Louis Calvert frowned, shaking his head. "You picked a bad man to tangle with, son. Jordan was quite a beloved man. . . ."

"Beloved, hell. He was a robber."

"He hid it well," Calvert said. "This very theater was founded by him. Half the men in town were his friends. I understand he and Sheriff McConnel came out from the East together." The older man shook his head. "No matter. I can't throw you to the dogs."

"I've tried every way out of town," Bandelier

253

said. "They've got the roads blocked and the river watched."

A devilish amusement lit Calvert's eyes suddenly. "You been in California two years, you say? Speak any Mexican?"

"Quite a bit. I worked with some Mexican miners."

"The Calvert Players are leaving for Downieville tonight on the stage," said Calvert. "Our second lead got the gold fever in 'Frisco last week and jumped the company. What do you think the good Sheriff McConnel would say if we went through his road block with a new actor in our troop named . . . ah . . . Montoyo Gonzales?"

For a moment, Bandelier stared suspiciously at him. Then he could not help the grin that spread across his face, the first humor he had felt in days.

"*Señor*," he said. "You have just hired a new second lead."

Inside, the stagehands were still striking the sets, and Calvert led Bandelier through the hustle to his dressing room. He gave Bandelier his razor, and while the younger man shaved himself, Calvert unlocked the wardrobe trunk. He pulled forth a pair of Mexican *charro* pants made of red suede with gold frogs sewed down the seam.

"We used these in *Knights of Old Madrid*," he said. "Here's a bullfighter's hat. I guess it'll look enough like the lids these *Californios* wear to pass muster. Now for some spirit gum, and a mustache. . . ."

A knock at the door cut him off, and a feminine voice called: "Are you decent, Uncle?"

Before Calvert could answer, the portal was pushed open, and the girl stepped inside. Tall, slim, deliciously curved, she stood with all the unconscious poise of a trained actress. Bandelier must have seen plenty of gold during his years in California. It could not match the color of her hair, clustered into a shimmering mass of curls beneath the brim of her poke bonnet. Against the clear pallor of her skin, her great blue eyes were startling. She stared blankly at him a moment, and then he saw the change harden her face.

"Uncle"—she threw her hand at Bandelier— "this . . ."

"Is Raymond Bandelier, the famous Raymond Bandelier, of Wallack's, New York, my dear. *Hamlet* and the *Merchant of Venice*. . . ."

"And the murderer of Henry Jordan in Sacramento," she finished hotly.

Calvert stepped forward, catching her hand placatingly. "Now, Persia, my dear . . ."

"What are you doing, Uncle Louis?" she asked, pulling away. "Surely you aren't . . . you can't . . ."

"We are!" thundered Calvert, in an imperious voice. "He says he didn't do it. I'm giving him the benefit of the doubt. We can't throw a fellow trouper to the dogs."

A faint thread of contempt rode Persia's voice. "A fellow trouper?"

Bandelier realized he was still holding the razor up, and lowered it. "What do you mean by that?"

"I saw you do *Hamlet*, too, Mister Bandelier," she said thinly. "Uncle Louis dragged me to it three times. I can't understand why they didn't stop booking you long before they did. You hardly moved your hands. Your face might as well have been carved from wood."

"You look intelligent," Bandelier told her sharply. "I should think you'd realize that mugging and gesturing are going out. Its high time we stopped waving at the gallery with every line. The time will come when your type of acting will make *Hamlet* look like comedy."

Calvert groaned. "You two really run true to form, don't you? The whole town is after this boy and you take time out to discuss technique."

Persia tossed her head. "I don't care, Uncle Louis. Bad actor or good, this man's still a murderer, and I won't let you help him escape."

"And what if he wasn't?" Calvert threw out his hand in a dramatic gesture. "What if they hanged him, and we found out afterward they had made a mistake. Could you ever face yourself in a mirror, Persia? Could you throw him to the dogs while there's still a doubt?"

She tried to hide the break in her anger. "He'll

never be able to put up a good enough act to get by that sheriff."

"At least give him the chance to try. He's going to be our new second lead. *Señor* Montoyo Gonzales, from Mexico City."

She almost laughed. "You couldn't have picked a worse part. Mexicans are grandiloquent, you know. They gesture and declaim. With Bandelier's passion for underplaying, he'll have Sheriff McConnel tearing off that fake mustache in a minute."

For the first time, Calvert's voice was quiet. "We're already accomplices, you know, Persia. We've already helped him."

She stared at him a moment. "You fool!" she said hotly, and wheeled to walk out.

Calvert stared after the slammed door, then shook his head. "I'm afraid your disguise isn't the only thing we have to worry about, my boy."

Bandelier met the actors before they walked the block to the stage station. There was the buxom, kindly character woman, and Sam Dent, the comedian. The ingenue was a shrew-faced, washed-out blonde, and the leading man was a tall, supercilious-looking young man named Herbert Kendall. They expressed surprise that Calvert should choose a Mexican, but he smoothed it over with his thunderous dramatics and herded them out.

It was a tight squeeze to get the whole troupe into the coach, and Bandelier found himself wedged in between Persia and her uncle on the back seat. There was still an angry, sullen look to Persia's narrowed eyes as they rolled out past the Union office, its oil lamps still going as the paper went to press. Then they were rattling through the hay-filled city market, and into the outskirts of town. And with every lurch of the coach, Bandelier found the tension in him mounting. He did not know exactly where the road would be blockaded, but it should be soon.

Then there was a shout from ahead, and a lantern swinging its saffron glow back and forth in the darkness. Thorough braces shrieked as the driver drew the coach to a halt. There was some talk outside, and then the door was swung open, and Sheriff Ewing McConnel leaned inside.

He held the lantern above his head to light the interior of the coach, so that his hat brim cast the top part of his face into black shadow, from which his eyes gleamed like the business ends of two Colts,

"Ah yes," he said. "Louis Calvert. I saw *Uncle Tom's Cabin* last night. Allow me to congratulate you, sir. I hate to cause you all this trouble, but we're hunting a murderer."

The sheriff's eyes jumped around the passengers one by one, seeming to flicker as they rested upon Bandelier. Calvert threw up his arm in a dramatic gesture.

"I don't understand you, sir. Obviously there is no one in here but my troupe. We're nothing but a group of simple actors going about our business of bringing a touch of civilization to this barbarous land. . . ."

Bandelier felt his hand on the window strap draw up with increasing tension. As each rolling syllable left Calvert's lips, McConnel's eyes seemed to grow more narrow with suspicion.

"Moreover, sir, you are holding up the United States mails. I'm sure you're aware what a felony that is."

"Take it easy, Calvert," McConnel broke in sharply. "There's nothing to get excited about." He glanced at Bandelier. "I didn't see you in the play last night."

"He's our new second lead," Calvert orated. "All the way from Mexico City. A man of international fame. One of the greatest . . ."

"Why not let him speak for himself?" asked McConnel impatiently.

Bandelier met the sheriff's eyes calmly, and spoke in a soft, casual voice. "My name is Montoyo Gonzales, *señor jerif*. I was honored with an offer to play in the distinguished Calvert Stock company when their second lead jumped the show in San Francisco. I only arrived here this evening."

"You ain't got much of an accent."

"Do you expect a *peon, señor*?"

McConnel's hat brim hid his whole face, with the downward tip of his head. "I beg your pardon, *señor.* . . ."

"Sheriff," said Persia, leaning forward sharply.

McConnel's brim lifted again, revealing those bright eyes. "Ma'am?"

Persia remained bent forward, a mingling of expressions filling her face. A horse stirred restlessly outside. Persia's eyes swung to Bandelier. Anger tinted her cheeks. Then she settled back, forcing a rueful little laugh.

"I guess I'm just nervous. We've heard Reboe Ayers has been holding up stages again."

McConnel hesitated, staring narrow-eyed at her. Then he stepped back, touching his hat brim. "Reboe's only interested in the gold coming down from the mines, ma'am." The door shut with a slam. "All right, Hack. Whip 'em up."

The coach lurched, and Calvert sank back, whipping out his handkerchief. " 'Now sure's the moment I ought to die, lest some hereafter bitterness impair this joy,' " he panted, mopping his brow. "Holy Beelzebub! I thought he was going to string us up."

"He would certainly have done something if you'd kept up that tirade," said Kendall, the leading man. "What did you think you were doing . . . *King Lear*! You were making him suspicious."

"Was I?" Calvert's pouched eyes widened in surprise. A vague, hurt look crossed his face. Then something sly filtered in. "Maybe you're right." His roguish eyes swung around to his niece. "Maybe I should have underplayed it, like Mister Gonzales."

II

Bandelier arrived at the dressing room he shared with Calvert at eight o'clock the night they opened in Downieville, to find that the older man was not there. Bandelier began putting on the dove-colored trousers he wore in *The Prairie Wife*. Every now and then the floor shuddered as Sam Dent practiced his falls in the next room. Bandelier was about to put on his frilled stock when the door opened and Louis Calvert came staggering in. He tripped over an open trunk and half fell into an arm chair.

"Louis, you old fool," Bandelier said. "Don't you know we go on in half an hour?"

Calvert's facile mouth formed a silly grin. "I'll be all right," he said, grinning broadly.

"With a bucket of ice water," snapped Bandelier. He got the bucket of water they had been using to wash in and put it before Calvert. "Now dip your head in."

Calvert started to protest. Bandelier grabbed him, forcing that shaggy, leonine head forward between Calvert's knees and down into ice-cold water taken straight from the North Yuba. When he released the man, Calvert reared up, sputtering like a walrus.

" 'The devil damn thee black, thou cream-faced loon!' " he roared. " 'Go . . . ,' " he trailed off, shaking his head. Then he sank back. "I forget the rest," he mumbled. His chin sank onto his chest, and he sprawled there in the chair, staring blankly before him, while Bandelier pulled the ever-present pot of coffee over the flame of their little woodstove.

"Thanks, son," Calvert said at last. "That did clear my head a little. Hate to have Persia see me in this condition." He shook his head sadly. "I guess you wonder why I act this way. You've been with us four days since Sacramento and seen me drunk three of them."

"I figured it was something in your past. You never married?"

Calvert snorted disgusted. "Nothing as easy as a broken love affair. You see before you a failure, Ray. Thrown to the dogs, playing the sticks. I would be in New York now, Wallack's. Star billing. If they'd only let me do it the way I wanted." He seemed to shrink in the chair, staring off into that distance, and his voice became very soft. "Underplaying, Ray. No more gestures, no more ham, no more licking the boots of the gallery gods."

Bandelier's eyes narrowed, and he almost whispered it. "You too?"

Calvert looked up with a small, rueful laugh. "Why do you think I'd seen so many of your plays? I've had the same idea as you for half my life, son. It's time for a change in the theater. All this melodrama has to go. But I didn't have what it takes. I tried again and again to put it across, and failed. I guess I've been hamming so long, I couldn't underplay if I had to. I nearly ruined it for you with McConnel, didn't I?"

Bandelier stared at Calvert, seeing him in a wholly different light, as he realized how the old man had been smashed by failure of the same dream he himself had cherished for so long. It gave him a poignant sense of rapport with Calvert, in that moment. Perhaps Calvert felt it. His head jerked up, his bleary eyes focused on Bandelier.

"Sure," he said. "Why do you think I was so quick to help you? Our bond goes deeper than the mere profession, boy. I don't want it to ruin you the way it's ruined me. You're pretty close to it now, aren't you? You failed in New York and you've come out here to fail again."

Bandelier felt his head lower as the bitterness of his defeat returned to him. "I guess so. It was getting so I couldn't find a booking any place back East. I thought it would be easier out here. It was worse. I finally had to take up prospecting to exist."

"You're still pretty rusty, having trouble picking up your lines."

"It isn't only that I've lost my confidence," Bandelier told him. "If Persia would only quit riding me. I'd think, being your niece, she'd understand what I'm trying to do."

"That's the point, son. She saw it ruin me. She saw me laughed off the stages of New York. The worst part of it is, you'll have to go along with her. The bulk of the public will have to be educated to underplaying before they'll accept it. These miners want ham. All I have to do is throw up my arm and bellow at the gallery and they cover the stage with bags of gold." He broke off, smiling ruefully. "I'm sorry. I didn't mean to give you another tirade."

"I understand." Bandelier smiled.

Calvert came over to catch his arm. "I think you do. That's why I want so to help you. Have you been able to remember anything else about what happened in Jordan's office? Any clue that might give us a lead to who really did it. The way I heard it, people in neighboring offices saw you go into Jordan's office about five. They heard the shots about six and ran in to find Jordan dead and somebody going out the window."

"But I only stayed in his office for ten minutes.

I must have left about ten after five. Surely somebody saw me go."

"Nobody's come up who did. It leaves you in a hole."

"He'll be in a deeper hole if he doesn't come out and at least try to rehearse those lines," Persia said, from the doorway.

Bandelier wheeled to stare in surprise, and then crossed in front of Calvert to hide the man's condition, closing the door behind him and following Persia out onto the stage. Here she turned to him.

"Now. You're over by the table. You're a rich planter's son who wants to marry me. You can't understand why I prefer a poor farmer to you. Please try to get a little anger, a little frustration into your voice. For just once, forget about your natural school. To me, it's just a name to cover a lack of technique."

A flush rose into his face. "All right. I can't understand why you want to marry a poor farmer. But I can understand why you hate natural acting." He found himself walking toward her. "You're afraid to give me a chance. You're afraid I'll show you up for the ham you are."

"That's the last time you'll call me a ham!" she said hotly.

He caught her hand before the slap could land. Perhaps it was that beneath all the antipathy he felt toward her, he still could not deny what her beauty did to him. He found himself pulling her close, kissing her fiercely. Then he let her go.

"How's that for anger?" he asked.

She stood staring at him a moment longer. Then, with a small sound of rage, she wheeled and walked to the wings.

The theater was filled at eight-thirty. Persia and Louis Calvert had the bulk of the first scene, and Bandelier watched from the wings. Toward the end of the act, some late-comers made a stir in the crowd. An immense, red-bearded man appeared in the door at the upper end of one aisle, surveying the crowd from beneath the down-tilted brim of his black slouch hat.

Then it was a narrow, grimy man in a great sombrero, with a livid knife scar running from eye to mouth. He looked to be one of the men from Chile who had come north to work the mines. At this moment, Persia brought the house down with her curtain line. Roaring and shouting, the miners rose in their seats, raining coins and pokes of gold dust on the stage, as was their custom when a play pleased them. It was a big crowd, and the money and bags of dust piled up until there must have been thousands of dollars on the stage. The gigantic redhead walked down the aisle, a handful of coins in his hand, as if to throw them at Persia. But when he reached the footlights, he climbed up over them. Before

266

anyone realized his intent, he had pulled a big Navy revolver from its holster beneath his long coat.

"Just keep your seats!" he roared. "We're taking this gold and whatever else you've got on you. Throw it out into the aisles. And don't try to keep your watches."

A bedlam of roaring and shouting lifted from the miners. There was a violent little stir from a seat on the aisle, near the rear. Before this movement finished, a shot made its deafening explosion in the room. A miner reared up from that seat on the aisle, his gun still half lifted toward the redhead on the stage. Then he pitched onto his face in the aisle.

It was only then that Bandelier saw the Mexican dressed in a gaudy *charro* outfit, standing in the rear door behind the Chileno, and blowing smoke from the tip of his gun.

"Anybody else want to try hees luck, now ees the time, *señores*," he called.

"It sure is," laughed the redhead, and started emptying his gun at the footlights. The miners in the front rows began scrambling to the aisles for safety. But the man was only darkening the stage so he would be a poorer target. When his gun was empty, it left but one footlight burning, casting the stage into deep shadow. A pair of men stepped from the wings and began gathering up the pokes of gold dust and money and stuffing them in the saddlebags they carried. Then they jumped off the stage into the aisles and picked up the sacks and pokes the men had thrown here, while the Mexican and the Chileno held the crowd at bay. The redhead finished reloading his gun, and walked over to Persia, swinging an arm around her waist before she could jump away.

"I think you'll ride along with Reboe a piece, little gal. They won't be so eager to follow if they know it will mean you get hurt."

Louis Calvert was near his niece, and he caught at Reboe's arm. "Now, look here, you red-headed buffoon. . . ."

"Lay off, old man!" shouted Reboe, swinging his arm around without releasing Persia, and bringing it in against Calvert so viciously the actor was knocked over backward. This wheeled the redhead away from where Bandelier still stood in the wings. The actor took his chance, jumping out at the man, hands outstretched to hook that gun arm. But he had not seen the curtain rope coiled on the floor. It snarled his left foot, tripping him headlong. Reboe wheeled back, gun lifting up. Then he saw what had happened, and threw back his head to laugh.

"You must be the comedian!" he shouted. "I wish we could take you along for laughs."

In that last moment, Bandelier raised his head dazedly to see the intense disappointment and disgust in Persia's face as she looked down at him. Then Reboe caught her up and swung her over his shoulder as easily as if she had been half her weight. Holding her there with one arm, he dropped off the stage and followed his men up the aisle, stooping now and then to snatch up a watch thrown into the aisle which his men had overlooked. The Chileno and the Mexican kept the crowd at bay till a few minutes after Reboe had disappeared, then they too ran out.

Seething with humiliation, Bandelier followed the rush of miners up the aisle. They were all running over that man who had been killed near the rear, and Bandelier halted here to scoop the Colt from his hand. Firing had already broken out on the street, from the miners who were now in the open. But Reboe and his men had already swung around a corner and disappeared. The only one in sight, as Bandelier ran across the sidewalk, was the Mexican. He was several buildings down, still fighting to mount an excited horse. The miners were firing at him, but they were as excited as the animal, and had not hit the man yet. Bandelier jumped off the curb with both feet, to halt his impetus, and waited till the jar of landing was over, and then fired. The Mexican had just swung up at the saddle, his right leg still in mid-air. He hung that way a moment, then fell back into the street, with the horse galloping off. Calvert was at Bandelier's side now, staring blankly at the Mexican.

"You didn't tell me you could shoot like that, Ray."

"Man has to learn more than prospecting to stay alive in these hills. I found I had a great talent for it, and I practiced incessantly," Bandelier told him grimly. "We've got to stop these miners from going after Persia, Louis."

Some of the men had spread out along the hitch rack to get horses, and Calvert turned their way, shouting at them. "Don't do that! They'll kill my niece if you follow. Didn't you hear what the redhead said?"

The mounted men swung their horses to a stop in the middle of the street, frowning at Calvert. Then, as the full implications of what he had said struck them, horsebackers drew their fiddling mounts in around Calvert.

"What'll we do?" one of them asked. "We can't just let them get away!"

Bandelier moved down toward the Mexican that had been killed. A few of the men followed, drawn by his movement. Bandelier frowned down at the body, something working in his mind. "The bandits didn't see this man killed, did they?" he asked.

"No," answered a miner. "They were all on around the corner."

Calvert had moved over, staring at Bandelier. "Ray, what's on your mind?"

"If I could masquerade as one Mexican, I can

do it as another," said Bandelier. "The stage was dark. Reboe didn't get a very good look at me. This Mexican's about my height and build."

As he finished, the gathering crowd parted again before the pressure of a ridden horse, and Bandelier looked up to see Sheriff Ewing McConnel sitting the saddle above him.

"It's lucky you come, Sheriff," said one of the men. "Reboe Ayers just held up the theater."

McConnel spoke without taking his gimlet eyes off Bandelier. "How do you know it was Reboe? I heard he was down by Marysville."

"He got all our watches. That's his trademark, ain't it? I've heard he has hundreds of 'em."

"Your own sheriff can handle that," answered McConnel. "I came after this man."

"But, Sheriff," Bandelier answered. "I am *Señor . . .*"

"Ray Bandelier," finished McConnel. "One of the stagehands in the Sacramento theater saw you go in Calvert's dressing room as a Yankee and come out a Mexican. He didn't tie it up at first, but I got around to questioning him day before yesterday."

Calvert thundered: "This town isn't in your county. You haven't got any official capacity here!"

McConnel leaned forward, voice bitterly deliberate. "My capacity is that Henry Jordan and I came here together from the East. He put

271

me in this office. Whatever his faults, he was my friend, and I'm taking back his murderer."

Bandelier caught at McConnel's stirrup leather. "Listen, Sheriff. Reboe's taken Persia Calvert as hostage. They'll kill her if a posse goes after her."

"If it's that bad, I'll go after them alone," said McConnel. "But first I'll see you in this town's calaboose."

"You're too well known," Bandelier insisted. "You couldn't get within ten miles of them. I won't argue with you about my innocence in the Jordan murder. All I ask is this one chance to go after Persia. I'll disguise myself as this dead Mexican. If I fail, you can have me."

"I'll put myself in your custody, Sheriff," offered Calvert, dramatically. "If Ray doesn't return, you can hold me as an accomplice to Jordan's murder. After all, I did help Bandelier escape."

McConnel stared in surprise at Calvert. "That's quite a recommendation from you."

"I have that much faith that Bandelier isn't a murderer, and that he can get my niece where nobody else can," answered Calvert. "Her life depends on it, Sheriff."

McConnel settled heavily into the saddle, frowning to himself. Absently he took a smashed coin from his pocket, and began to flip it. Finally he spoke.

"All right. I'm a damned fool, but all right."

"We'd better get you made up," Calvert said, grabbing Bandelier's arm. Then he wiped at his brow and tried to laugh in a pathetic attempt at his habitual theatrics. "Beelzebub! Edwin Booth never got a chance to play a part like this!"

III

Bandelier had spent enough time in the mountains these last two years to pick up some tracking. He followed the bandits from Downieville, well enough, in the moonlit night. They turned off the road near Comptonville, however, crossed a stream, and he lost the tracks.

It was then that he had to take a chance. During his time prospecting through the Sierras, he had heard many tales of Reboe Ayers. One of his favorite stopping places and hide-outs was supposed to be the Florida House, set up on the dizzying heights above Goodyear's Bar, along one of the least accessible sections of the Downieville Road. Bandelier stopped tracking and headed straight through Comptonville, on up the road, to reach the Florida House near midnight that night.

It was a two-story log structure with a tall hip roof and a chimney at either end. There was no one about outside, but Bandelier saw half a dozen horses in the corral covered with the briny mottling of dried sweat. He hitched his animal at the rack in front and stepped up on the porch and through the door. The great taproom was empty, save for the bartender, who looked up in surprise.

"Lola!" called the barman sharply.

There was the shudder of stairs, and a voluptuous Mexican woman appeared in the hall, flounced skirt swinging. This was Lola Salazar, the mistress of the Florida House. There was nothing sinister in the smile that broke over her dark face now, however.

"Peso!" she cried, running forward and flinging the arms about him in a hug that would have made a mother bear ashamed. "We thought you had been shot or something!"

"My horse was shot out from under me," he told her in Spanish. "Are the others here?"

"In the back room," she told him, leading him down the hall and flinging open a heavy door on one side to reveal another taproom. This was a filthy den, littered with riding gear and blankct rolls, a long split-log table running down the center, about which sat half a dozen men. At the head, just setting down a tankard he had drained, was Reboe Ayers.

"Peso!" he bawled, rising to his feet. "We thought they'd got you for sure. Come here and sit between the Chileno and me. Lola, tell that lazy muck of a husband to get our pard some food and drink. And where's the girl? I told you to bring her down."

"She is tired," protested Lola.

"Bring her down!" shouted Reboe, pounding on the table with his tankard.

Lola looked at him resentfully, then turned to flounce out. Meanwhile, Bandelier had seated himself beside the dark, scarred man from Chile, who was already grinning foolishly with drink. The candle lighting this end of the table was set in a tin sconce beside a bowl of bread. Bandelier saw Reboe frowning at him narrowly, and reached out to grab for the bread, allowing his arm to strike the candle. It went over, sputtering against the table, to go out.

"Hell!" shouted a man from across the table. "Now I can't see to eat."

"Don't be crazy," the Chileno laughed. "It's light as day, ain't it, Peso? Show us how."

He tossed a coin into the air. Bandelier glanced up at it blankly. Reboe bent drunkenly toward him.

"What's the matter, Peso? Losing your touch?"

Bandelier remembered that smashed coin McConnel had been flipping in Downieville. It tied in, somehow, but he did not understand yet. He shook his head wearily.

"I guess I'm just tired. They got my horse. I had to hide out in town a couple of hours."

Reboe was staring intently at him. "What happened to your hair? Get it cut?"

Bandelier raised his head to see the suspicion in the man's eyes. Before he could answer, the door opened again, and Lola ushered Persia Calvert in.

Her face was taut with strain, but her eyes met the men's defiantly. Reboe made a guttural sound of appreciation deep in his throat, and rose to lurch down the table to the girl.

"Now, little actress," he said. "We want some entertainment. Give Reboe a kiss and I'll let you get up on the table and dance for us."

He tried to swing her around and kiss her, but she blocked him off with an arm, struggling violently. It was all Bandelier could do to contain himself. Suddenly one of Persia's hands flashed up, clawing across Reboe's eye. He jumped back. "You little witch!" he roared.

Bandelier stepped in front of the man, as he lurched back toward Persia. "Maybe she do better with couple of drinks," he said.

Reboe swayed back and forth, suspicion tightening his single good eye. But he was just drunk enough to find the sudden, illogical humor in that, and he began to chuckle.

"You're right, Peso," he said, and wheeled heavily toward the table. The whiskey was at the other end, and he shouted for the Chileno to bring it to him. Persia had backed over against the wall, and it gave Bandelier that instant to move over by her.

"How about underplaying now, Persia?" he muttered. "Or would you rather I hammed it up and got our throats slit?" He saw shock widen her eyes. Then a wild relief slackened her whole face, parting the lips. She breathed his name. "Yes," he said. "It's Bandelier. Tell me quick. What's this about Peso? The coin they toss up."

"I heard them talking." Her voice was a tense whisper. "He shoots it. Nine out of ten."

"I've done my share of shooting," Bandelier told her.

Reboe's voice welled up out of the babble of the other men. "What the hell are you talking about?"

Bandelier turned to face him with that faint smirk. "What would any man talk about, *amigo*, with a woman such as this?"

Reboe grabbed his wrist in a grip that compressed Bandelier's lips with the pain. "You ain't cutting in on me, Peso. Leave the girl alone."

Still smiling, Bandelier asked: "Would you like me to shoot your ears off?"

That suspicion glittered in Reboe's eyes. "How could you do that if you can't even hit this?"

With his free hand he had fished a coin from his pocket, tossing it in the air. It took Bandelier by surprise, and Reboe still gripped his left wrist.

Unable to turn toward the coin, Bandelier had to pull and shoot off to the side, with only the barest glance at the coin winking its brazen path through the feeble light. He fired once, and the Chileno pounced for the coin as it struck the floor, and held it up to the light.

"You better hide your ears, Reboe," he said. "It's been hit."

Reboe still gripped Bandelier's wrist, staring into his face, and Bandelier knew he had to turn his mind from this quickly. "Speaking of smashed coins," he said. "McConnel was in Downieville about something while I was hiding out there. He had a smashed coin he kept flipping."

Reboe's eyes widened. "You didn't drop one in Jordan's office, did you?"

Bandelier tried to hide the sudden tension that stiffened his body. "Why would I do a stupid thing like that?" he asked. He shrugged, grinning at the man, and took a shot in the dark. "It wouldn't pin anything on me if I did."

"You were with me!" Reboe's voice raised to a guttural shout. "You can't get out of that!"

With a sudden vicious jerk, Bandelier pulled his wrist free of Reboe's hand. "Why do we get so excited about one little killing?" he said. "Are you having bad dreams?"

Reboe let out a disgusted laugh. "You'll have them before I do." He seemed to remember the girl. A leer swept the anger from his face, as he turned to her. "Give her a drink. She looks pale." The Chileno had been standing by with a bottle and cups, and he poured Persia a shot. She held the cup out from her, staring at it disgustedly.

"Come on," snarled Reboe impatiently. "You was doing better than this on the stage."

"*Si.*" Bandelier smiled. "She is a marvelous actress. I see her down in Marysville last year when the Calvert company was there. I particular like the last scene in that play about the plowman. Remember, *señorita*?"

She met his eyes, as if sensing he was trying to get something across to her. Then she forced a smile.

"I remember," she said, and lifted the liquor to her lips.

"That's better!" chortled Reboe. "Empty it up, and give me a kiss."

She choked on it, spat half of it out. Then she dropped the tin cup and sagged against the wall, a hand fluttering to her head.

"I feel dizzy," she moaned.

Reboe laughed. "You ought to."

He made a grab for her. She moaned again, turning aside from him to crumple to the floor. It was even more convincing than the faint she had done in *The Plowman's Daughter*.

"Now see what you've done!" shrieked Lola, rushing between them to kneel beside Persia. "I

279

told you she was delicate. You've made her sick with that atrocious stuff. Eduardo, help me carry this poor little pigeon upstairs."

Lola's husband came scurrying from the hall, and between them they carried Persia out. Reboe stared after them in drunken befuddlement. He turned to frown at Bandelier. Then he stumbled back to the table, cursing obscenely, and flung himself into the chair. The other men were raising a drunken, shouting hubbub now. Bandelier joined them. It took a long time for liquor and exhaustion to take effect.

One by one, however, they fell asleep.

He found the stairs in a pitch black hall, rising to an upper hall lighted by one pine-knot torch. Lola's narrowed stooped husband stood before a door. Bandelier found cigarette papers in the pockets of Peso's pants, began rolling one as he walked up to the man.

"How's the girl?"

"Sleeping. You can't get in. Lola told me nobody was to get in."

"At least give me a light, Eduardo."

The man's eyes dropped as he fished in his pocket. Bandelier pulled his gun. Eduardo tried to jerk his hand free. Bandelier caught him on the side of the neck with the barrel before he could block it. Bandelier stepped over his body, into the room.

"Persia?"

A bed squeaked, the floor trembled, she was in his arms. "Ray, Ray . . ."

"No time for talk. We've got to get out."

He led her through the silent house to a back door, and across the stony compound to a corral. He saddled up for her, helped her on. Then he caught one bareback, taking no time to put a saddle on for himself. At this moment, Lola's voice rang out from within the house.

"Eduardo, Eduardo! What have they done to you? Reboe!"

There were rattling sounds from the lower floor, a thick voice shouting. Bandelier and Persia had to round the house to the front to gain the trail that led to the road. As they clattered around by the porch, the front door was flung open, and the Chileno ran into the moonlight, brandishing a gun. Bandelier shot first. It caught the Chileno up and carried him back against the wall. He was still hanging there, as if spitted, when a man with a revolving Colt rifle appeared. Bandelier flung a pair of shots at him. The man ducked back inside, shouting something. Bandelier and the girl were out of range, now. As the house dropped from view, Bandelier saw Reboe come to the door, look after them, then wheel to head for the corral.

"He may catch us," she said. "There's a cut-off leading into the house from lower on the Downieville road. I heard them talking about it. They can head us off!"

"Then flog up your horse!" he called to her.

Desperately they galloped down the narrow, winding trail. After a mile it struck the Downieville road. Bandelier wheeled southward there, hoping they could pass that cut-off before any of the gang.

A great black shape burst suddenly from what looked like a gully cut in the slope ahead. Persia's horse veered aside, almost going over the cliff. Bandelier could not turn that way without knocking her on over, so he went head-on into the shape.

The sudden smashing blow pitched him over his horse's head. He had the glimpse of another horse. Then he was going into the rider, carrying him off, with the squeal of animals rising shrilly from behind. Bandelier hit, grappled with the other man, and they rolled over twice.

Dazed, Bandelier tried to tear from underneath the other man. But the man raised above him, a dim shape in the darkness, with a great beard blotting out the bottom of his face. Reboe Ayers.

"Damn you, Peso," he snarled. "Trying to steal the gal!"

He smashed down with a blow that would have finished it then. But Bandelier threw up an arm to block it and jerked aside. Reboe's fist glanced off his forearm and went into the earth, with Reboe coming heavily against him. The man was off balance in that instant, and Bandelier got a shoulder under him, and heaved him over.

Reboe grappled the actor against him as they rolled. Coming on top of the man and unable to raise up in Reboe's grip, Bandelier caught his beard, smashing Reboe's head against the rocks.

Reboe shouted and rolled on over with Bandelier. The actor could not keep the man's greater weight from carrying him over and under. But he managed to get a leg splayed out, and kept them rolling.

When he came up on top of Reboe once more, he smashed the man's head against the rocks again. The slope steepened, and they kept rolling. Each time he came up, Bandelier beat the man's head into the stone-studded earth that way. About the fifth time around, Reboe's arms were no longer holding Bandelier. Sucking in great, gasping breaths, Bandelier got to his hands and knees. He saw that no breath stirred Reboe's chest.

Persia had halted her horse and swung off down the road, and was running back up to him. Swaying there, he held out the watch.

"Think this'll clinch the case for McConnel?"

"If he'd found a smashed coin in Jordan's office, he must have already begun to suspect the possibility of your innocence," she said. "I don't think he would have let you come up here otherwise."

"I guess you're right. I'd been talking to a lot

of miners about being grub-staked by Jordan. Reboe must have heard how much money Jordan meant to give me, and followed me to his office that day." Bandelier glanced back of them. "We'd better take off. If none of the others have come out of that cut-off by now, it must mean they took the long way after us. That'll give us a few minutes. When they find Reboe dead, I doubt if they'll come on after us." He wheeled back, catching her elbows. "You'll back me up by telling McConnel what Reboe said about murdering Jordan?"

"I'll tell McConnel everything," she murmured. "I'll tell him how wonderful your new school of acting is. I didn't even know it was you till you told me. I'll never ham again, Ray. But there's one thing I never want you to underplay."

"What's that?"

"This."

Her lips were cool at first. Then warm. She was right. It was something he would never underplay.

Additional Copyright Information:

About the Author

Les Savage, Jr. was born in Alhambra, California and grew up in Los Angeles. His first published story was "Bullets and Bullwhips" accepted by the prestigious magazine, Street & Smith's *Western Story*. Almost ninety more magazine stories followed, all set on the American frontier, many of them published in Fiction House magazines such as *Frontier Stories* and *Lariat Story Magazine* where Savage became a superstar with his name on many covers. His first novel, *Treasure of the Brasada* appeared from Simon & Schuster in 1947. Due to his preference for historical accuracy, Savage often ran into problems with book editors in the 1950s who were concerned about marriages between his protagonists and women of different races—a commonplace on the real frontier but not in much Western fiction in that decade. Savage died young, at thirty-five, from complications arising out of hereditary diabetes and elevated cholesterol. However, as a result of the censorship imposed on many of his works, only now are they being fully restored by returning to the author's original manuscripts. Among Savage's finest Western stories are *Fire Dance at Spider Rock* (1995), *Medicine Wheel* (1996), *Coffin Gap*

(1997), *In the Land of Little Sticks* (2000), and *Danger Rides the River* (2002). Much as Stephen Crane before him, while he wrote, the shadow of his imminent death grew longer and longer across his young life, and he knew that, if he was going to do it at all, he would have to do it quickly. He did it well, and, now that his novels and stories are being restored to what he had intended them to be, his achievement irradiated by his powerful and profoundly sensitive imagination will be with us always, as he had wanted it to be, as he had so rushed against time and mortality that it might be.

Center Point Large Print
600 Brooks Road / PO Box 1
Thorndike, ME 04986-0001 USA

(207) 568-3717

US & Canada:
1 800 929-9108
www.centerpointlargeprint.com